4112

Praise for the Shenanigans Series

"A fabulously fun series."
The Literary Word

"Oertel keeps the tension mounting...
leaving fans eager for the next installment."
Booklist

"A fun, engaging series for
adventure and history buffs."
Quill & Quire

"It is Nancy Drew meets *The Goonies* with a twist."
Children's Literature

"Two latter-day Hardy boys and a Nancy Drew
may just awaken the Indiana Jones in young readers
and teach a bit of history at the same time."
Kirkus Reviews

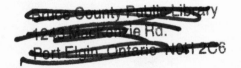

Bruce County Public Library
1243 Mackenzie Rd.
Port Elgin, Ontario N0H 2C6

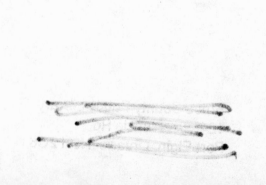

PROLOGUE

ISTHMUS OF PANAMA, 1513 AD

"WILL YOU FINISH the carving today?" Thiago asked his grandfather.

The old man ignored Thiago and wiggled his stool closer to the window, allowing the sunlight to fall directly on the skull again. The giant crystal seemed to gather the sun's rays and shoot them out as a thousand brilliant shards of light.

Thiago cleared his throat and tried once more. "Will it be ready today?"

His grandfather opened his hand and held it out to Thiago. "Perhaps," he said.

The thirteen-year-old boy's eyes widened, and he placed another pinch of fine sand in the middle of the callused palm. This was not the reply he usually heard—*Perhaps*. Could his grandfather finally be finished? *Perhaps*. What an amazing development!

His grandfather dropped the sand inside the left eye socket, spit on a small square of bat fur, and began polishing the quartz with his thumb. Thiago couldn't believe it. Today might be the day. After six years of work, the copy of the crystal skull may finally be ready. The skull on his grandfather's lap looked identical to the skull he had been replicating for months—at least to Thiago. But never to his grandfather.

"Perhaps," Thiago mumbled to himself, staring at the original skull on the pedestal under the window. He knew his grandfather's two previous attempts to replicate that skull had failed. His father had told him stories about those early copies and how the enormous crystals shattered after several years of painstaking work. The fragments from those experiments were buried under the work area where they sat. Thiago glanced down at the many layers of fur on the floor, meant to protect the skull should it ever slip from his grandfather's hands. And that had happened—at least four times—but the skull thankfully wasn't damaged.

Suddenly, his grandfather stopped polishing. He passed Thiago the new skull—the copy—and gently lifted the true skull with both hands. They sat side by side, each holding one of the human-sized crystal skulls. "Can you see a difference?" Grandfather asked.

"No," he quickly told his grandfather, "they look exactly the same."

Grandfather sighed. "Please examine them carefully, Thiago. They *must* be alike. My dreams were clear."

Thiago was ashamed. After the countless hours his grandfather spent creating the skull, he should at least pretend to scrutinize and compare the two pieces. He hefted the skull and held it close to his face. Rotating it slowly, he admired his grandfather's work.

The eyes were carved beautifully—spaced equally and set to the same depth as the original. The empty sockets stared back with guarded shadows that seemed to hold the same secrets locked inside the original skull. And the teeth—they alone had taken over a year—were a perfect match to the teeth in the skull resting in his grandfather's rough hands. They sparkled and grinned with menace at Thiago.

Not wanting to hear the story of his grandfather's dreams again, Thiago carefully swapped skulls with the old man and began examining the secret skull—the real skull. Sure, the stories of his grandfather's visions had enthralled and entertained him as a young boy, but he was thirteen now and almost a man.

Had Grandfather wasted all those years creating this copy? Thiago wondered, looking at the head. *Or did the spirits really demand he make a replica of this?*

His family and his village had always been responsible for protecting the skull, but it wasn't until Thiago was born that his grandfather's dreams began. In those dreams he was instructed to make a copy of the skull

3

they were protecting. Apparently, a fake skull would be needed to trick *a great foreigner* into leaving this village in peace. And they needed to be left in peace so that they could continue to guard the original skull until the day—

"Well?" grandfather asked, pulling him back to the present. "What do you think?"

Thiago decided to be honest. "The shape of the skull is a perfect match... but... but the crystal of your skull is slightly hazy compared with the true skull, which appears to be more pure—more clear."

Grandfather nodded.

"But you have matched its shape perfectly," Thiago repeated. "And no one will be able to identify the copy."

His grandfather began wrapping the fake skull in puma fur. "So you believe it will fool the Spanish?"

Thiago stopped trying to search for the skull's secret hidden deep within the crystal. "Yes, especially the Spanish. They should be easy to trick."

Although Thiago had never seen the strange people from across the water, he'd heard many fascinating stories from the other tribes that lived and traded along the narrow isthmus. The Chibchan people reported that the Spanish were loud and possessed enormous boats. The Maya from the northern forests said they were violent and greedy. But it was the Ahshmitohren who insisted the Spanish were dumb, describing how they wore steel hats and far too many clothes in the hot jungle. Thiago always thought that was especially funny because other tribes often joked that it was the Ahshmitohren who were not very bright.

Doctalubee, Thiago's uncle, had confirmed some of these observations only days ago. Upon his return to the village from a hunting trip, he reported excitedly that he saw many giant ships. Those ships stayed well away from shore, but smaller vessels were quickly lowered and used to ferry hundreds of Spanish to the beaches. "And," Doctalubee had said, "some were indeed wearing clothes made of shiny metal."

One of the youngest Spanish sailors had wandered off the beach and Doctalubee followed him. Feeling brave, he approached the lad and attempted to communicate with him. Perhaps the boy was sent to look for a water supply and Doctalubee could help. But the youth shook with fear and ran back to the beach. Thiago wished he could have been there to witness the encounter.

"When the Spanish come here," Grandfather pointed out the window at the stone homes of their small village, "we must be ready."

Thiago nodded. He knew what his grandfather intended to do.

But the old man repeated the plan anyway. "We will ask the Spanish not to curse our village with their evil ailments." He lightly touched the bumps on his forehead that had mysteriously appeared that day. "And in exchange, I will give them this magical skull." He tapped the fake skull and smiled at the boy.

"Just as your dream foretold, right, Grandfather?" Thiago asked. His tribe, the Chocoan, were the bravest people in the land, but they were terrified of the strange diseases the foreigners brought with them. If the stories were true, their horrible pox often reached villages long before they arrived—like the spreading smoke of a wildfire. "Their clouds of death will pass us over when they receive the new skull, yes?"

Grandfather shrugged. "That part of my vision was not clear," he admitted for the first time. "In my dreams I was told a powerful foreigner would be tricked with the skull. If not the Spanish and their foul ailments, who is there to deceive?"

Thiago didn't like the sound of that at all. His grandfather had always been confident in the meaning of his dreams and in the purpose of the fake skull, but now he didn't seem so sure.

The old man coughed violently and spat out the window. He didn't look well today. His face was pale and waxen, and the bumps on his head had formed blisters and were beginning to ooze an ugly pus.

A wave of fear suddenly washed over Thiago, and he wanted to change the subject. Still holding the real skull on his lap, he said, "Please show me the secret inside this skull again." He'd been twisting and turning the crystal, but he couldn't find the symbols.

"I will show you," his grandfather said weakly, "but first you must retell the story."

Thiago didn't think he'd be shown the skull's secret without having to recite the legend, but it was worth a try. Although Grandfather was old, he could not be fooled as easily as the Spanish or the Ahshmitohren.

"A long time ago," Thiago began, "a man appeared in our village with this skull and—"

"How long ago?" Grandfather interrupted.

Thiago thought for a moment. "One thousand, five hundred and ... and forty-eight moons ago."

He nodded. "And where was he found?"

"He arrived near the stones—near the three stone pillars." Thiago pointed outside and across the bay.

"Yes. Continue."

"The man gave our ancestors the skull and said we must keep it safe and protect it until it is needed. He said it can never be sold or traded. The man spoke our language, but very poorly. He said eight thousand full moons will come and go before its message can be understood, but when it is finally understood it will help all the tribes of all the world. The stranger said it must be protected until then."

"And *who* must keep this crystal skull safe?" Grandfather asked.

Thiago had been made to repeat the story many times and the words flowed from his mouth with little thought. "Our people, our village, our family."

The old man smiled. "Yes. Especially our family."

"Will you show me the proper way to hold it now?"

Thiago's grandfather took the skull and let the sun shine directly on the crystal forehead. A rainbow appeared on the mud-brick wall behind them. Thiago admired the colourful lines for a moment, but he had seen many natural rainbows and was more interested in seeing the symbols inside the skull. His grandfather turned the skull and examined the dent where an ear might be.

"There!" Grandfather said. "Look right there."

Thiago strained to see the tiny people he hadn't seen in months. "I can't see . . ."

"Don't try so hard," his grandfather said, steadying the skull with both hands. "Let your eyes relax . . . you will . . ."

"Yes!" Thiago hissed. "I see it now." The image of a man and a woman popped into focus and seemed to float inside the centre of the crystal. The colourful arc of a rainbow stretched over the two. "What does it mean?"

His grandfather pulled the skull away. "It does not matter *what* the message means. It only matters that we protect it." As he wrapped the special skull, the old man noticed more bumps appearing on his arms.

Thiago saw his grandfather was deep in thought, so he kept quiet.

"You are not scared of the forest or the jungle animals, are you?" Grandfather asked suddenly.

Thiago quickly shook his head. "No. I am brave like my father, and like you"

"Then I—" The old man coughed violently. "Then I," he began again, "have an important task for you."

"What is it?" Thiago asked, eager for a mission.

"I want you to take both skulls across the bay. Carry them to the three stones, hide them, and then wait there until someone comes for you. You may be alone for many days, but do not come back to the village unless . . . unless someone fetches you. Do you understand?"

Thiago did his best to hide his disappointment. The assignment didn't sound challenging at all. "Can I take Chachi and Kel-kel?" The trip would be a lot less dull, Thiago reasoned, if he could bring his two best friends.

The old man thought for a minute. "Yes, take them. But tell no one else. Now hurry. Go before nightfall." He gave Thiago both fur-wrapped packages and shooed him to the door. "And remember: the skulls must be protected— the future depends on it."

CHAPTER
1

"I'M MUCH TOO nervous to sit," Anna said. She lifted her legs, twisted away from the picnic table, and began pacing.

Rachel got up too. "Come on," she said to Anna, "we'll show you Cody's mom's flower garden. She has some amazing roses."

Eric stood up to join the girls, but I yanked on his elbow and held him back. When Anna and Rachel had drifted out of earshot, I said, "What did your mom say?"

Eric sat down again. "About going to Panama?"

"Yeah," I whispered. "You think she'll let you and Rachel go?"

"It's hard to say, Code. But she probably will if your mom and dad are okay with it."

"That's what I thought."

And *that's* why we were all a bit edgy. You see, Anna's dad, Dr. Bruno Wassler—I'll call him Bruno from now on—was meeting in my house with our parents at that very moment. He was trying to convince them to let us go to Panama with him and Anna. If we were allowed to go, we would all hook up with Rudi—that's Anna's uncle—who was already working there on some kind of archaeological project in the jungle.

Eric laughed. "My mom actually thought it was a joke when we told her we were invited on an archaeological trip. The emails proved we weren't making stuff up, but it wasn't till she spoke with your mom that she really took it seriously."

"Yeah," I said, "those emails were pretty official looking." I remembered my mom's face when she saw all the travel documents and letters of support that Anna's dad sent from Cambridge University. But what really surprised our parents was that he flew to Manitoba three days later (that is, today) to speak with them.

"I wonder how Bruno's interview is going?" Eric asked.

I automatically looked over at the house. "I wouldn't want to be in his shoes right now."

Bruno was a super nice, crazy-scientist-professor kind of guy, and I felt sorry for him. He'd have to do some pretty creative fibbing if our parents asked him why he wanted to take us on such a fancy field trip. I mean, he certainly couldn't say that we all became friends after jumping into a wormhole to save his daughter, Anna. Sure, that was true, and it had all worked out in the end, but it's just not the sort of story your average parent would believe.

I suspected Bruno was inviting us to Panama as a way of saying thanks, for when we travelled back in time and rescued Anna. Plus, he probably also knew we were interested in archaeology and would enjoy a trip to an archaeological dig. That's what archaeologists call big projects, by the way—digs.

Anyway, the three of us really wanted to travel with Anna, and we hoped Bruno could talk our parents into letting us go. I had wanted to stick around the house to hear their conversation, but Mom firmly suggested we go outside for a while.

Rachel and Anna returned to the picnic table and slipped back onto the benches.

"Anna flew here all the way from England," Rachel scolded, "and you guys are too lazy to walk around the yard with us."

"I'm saving my energy for Panama," Eric shot back smartly.

"You didn't even know *where* Panama was when we got Anna's first email," Rachel said. "I had to find it for you in the atlas."

"I knew it was a country somewhere in that pinched, narrow part—somewhere between North America and South America."

"That's why they call that area *Central* America," I suggested, helpfully. "It's between the two."

"Yeah, I knew Panama was in there somewhere," Eric said, "I just wasn't sure *exactly* which country it was."

"Riiiight," Rachel said.

"It's true." Eric blinked a few times like he always did when he wanted to look honest. "But all the names of the countries in that area sound the same."

"Okay," Rachel said, "name one."

"The Banana Republic," Eric said. "*Banana* sounds a lot like *Panama*."

"That is not a country, Eric," Anna said frowning. Her English was perfect, but she spoke it with a German accent, because that's where she was born—in Germany. Anna was the only person we knew who had travelled all over the world and lived in many countries. And right now she was living in England. "I believe that is a company that makes clothes."

We all laughed—especially Eric.

I looked at my watch and stood up. "Well," I said, "I suppose we should go inside and find out what they decided."

When we got to the back door, I took a deep breath and led my friends inside.

Dad was leaning against the kitchen counter with his arms folded tightly across his chest. Eric and Rachel's mom (Mrs. Summers), my mom, and Bruno were sitting around the kitchen table. Bruno looked hot and uncomfortable, and I don't think the coffee he was sipping was helping him cool down or relax. He dabbed at his upper lip with the handkerchief he held tight in his hand.

Everyone looked at us when we walked in.

I made eye contact with my mom and she held a finger to her lips. *Oops*, I thought, *we returned too soon.* I glanced at my dad. He was now squinting and rubbing his chin, thinking hard. Yup, we were interrupting something important.

Dad ignored us and said, "Okay, let me see if I have this all straight now. The contractors who have been working to widen and rebuild the Panama Canal recently found a bunch of interesting stuff."

Bruno nodded. "Very interesting artifacts—yes."

"So the work was immediately stopped," my dad continued, "and leading archaeologists from all over the world have been invited to come and investigate the area."

Anna's dad nodded again. "My brother Rudi was actually one of the first people contacted. He is already there... there at the site."

"And you're a professor of archaeology in England—at Cambridge? That's why you were asked to go?"

Another nod. "Yes, Rudi and I are both archaeologists."

"And you and your daughter are heading to Panama tomorrow, to work on the site?"

"Yes," Bruno said, "and I'd like to invite Cody, Eric, and Rachel to join us."

I held my breath.

My dad scratched his head. "You see," he said, "*that's* the part that has me confused. *Why* do you want to take our kids?"

"This should be interesting," Eric whispered in my ear.

Bruno cleared his throat and swiped at his damp forehead with the handkerchief. "Last month, when Anna was lost in the forest near here, it was your children who immediately went into the woods, heroically saving her."

"He's not kidding about that!" Eric said, obviously referring to our trip to the past and the ancient Cree village where we had stayed.

My dad heard Eric mumbling and frowned in our direction.

"Shhh," Rachel said.

Bruno continued: "I would like to show my appreciation for that kindness by inviting them on this trip."

"And you're actually willing to pay for the kids?" Dad asked. I guess he figured Bruno thanked us enough when we returned from the forest with Anna.

Bruno laughed lightly. "Well, to be honest," he said, "I won't be paying personally. But I am a founding member of the World Junior Archaeologists—the WJA—which is starting a program to get youth involved in archaeological field work. Anna tells me that Cody, Eric, and Rachel have an interest in history, and I will see that they are sponsored by Kids Dig It. That is the name of the program—Kids Dig It."

"And they're the ones paying for the trip?" That was Mrs. Summers. "The whole thing?"

"Yes," Bruno said, "and the timing couldn't be more perfect."

"Why's that?" Dad asked.

"Kids Dig It has been anxiously waiting for an *international* archaeological project that can be used to test the program. And Panama is it! Each country invited to participate in the canal discovery will also be sending four or five junior Kids Dig It members. I will be representing England, and I would love for your children to be my Kids Dig It delegates."

"But our kids are Canadian," Mrs. Summers said. "Will they allow three Canadian children on an English team?"

"For this project, yes," Bruno said. "Our Canadian contacts told us they don't have the time to assemble a proper delegation from Canada, so they encouraged me to include your children on my team."

"Wow!" my dad said. "Things have sure changed since I was young. When we went on field trips, we hopped on a school bus and drove to the museum. And that was it. No plane rides, no fancy hotels—"

"There will be no *fancy* hotels," Bruno said, cutting my dad off, "or *any* hotels, for that matter."

"What?" I said.

"Huh?" croaked Eric.

"To truly experience life as an archaeologist, the children will be working and living in the field. Of course there will be many other young people on the site, and the accommodations will meet recreational camp standards for health and safety, but there will be nothing fancy about their quarters."

Eric groaned and Rachel jabbed him in the ribs. But that only made him groan louder.

Dad grinned at us fiendishly. "Now *that* sounds more like it."

"Upon completion of their reports and presentations," Bruno added, "they can even apply for credit hours from the WJA."

"Reports!?" I asked.

"Presentations!?" Eric cried.

Our parents suddenly looked a whole lot happier, which I didn't like one bit. The trip was starting to sound more like an outdoor classroom than a fun holiday. I was about to say "forget it" when I suddenly realized Bruno might be making the camp sound more educational than it really was so that our parents would approve.

Anna's dad turned and looked at us. "You will be expected to treat the experience like a mini-course at school. You will take notes, document your findings, and then submit a field report of your experience to Kids Dig It."

"You can't be serious," Eric whined.

"Don't be rude, Eric," Mrs. Summers said sternly.

"And when you return to school," Bruno said, "you will make a presentation to your classmates and teachers. I'm sure they will enjoy hearing what you have to say. And then, each time you volunteer at a dig site, visit a museum, or explore a historical landmark, you may apply for additional credit hours from the World Junior Archae-ologists. When you have a certain number of hours, you will be awarded prizes for your commitment to the field. That is basically how the Kids Dig It program works—in an eggshell."

I think he meant *nutshell*, but no one corrected him.

"It all sounds very interesting," my dad concluded, "and we appreciate you coming here to speak to us in person."

Bruno smiled.

Dad looked at me. "Cody, please take Dr. Wassler outside for some fresh air, so we can talk for a minute."

Bruno bounced up from his seat and shooed us outside. I think he really did need some fresh air, the way he was pushing and shoving us. We went to the picnic table again and sat down.

Bruno's cell phone suddenly came alive with the ring tone from some weird German folk song. At first he looked like he was going to ignore it, but then he changed his mind and began groping around in his pockets for the device. He eventually found it, excused himself, and walked over to the shade of a big willow with the phone pressed to his ear.

I turned back to my friends. "Pu–leeease tell me your dad was kidding in the house," I begged Anna.

"About what?" she asked, looking bewildered.

"All of it," Eric said, "nothing he said in there sounds like fun."

Anna looked devastated. "I'm sorry, Eric, but that was all true." She glanced back over her shoulder at the kitchen window. "Well, except the part about how we met, of course."

"What's the problem?" Rachel asked, looking between me and her brother.

"Are you kidding?" Eric said, throwing up his arms. "I thought we were going on a fun trip, not to a summer bootcamp to do homework and reports and presentations. Yuck!"

"Does that mean you boys don't want to go to Panama?" Anna asked. She looked pretty disappointed too.

"No, I'm not saying that," I said. "It's just..."

"It's just that we do school stuff all year long," Eric said, "and we *don't* want to do assignments during our summer holidays. There! I said it!"

"Come on, you guys," Rachel pleaded. "Don't be such party poopers."

"Please come," Anna said. "I will help you with any assignments we are given. We can do everything as a team. It will be fun. Just like when we were in old Sultana."

"I suppose that would make it more fun," I admitted.

"And the next time," Anna said, "we can fly wherever you want."

"What do you mean?" Rachel asked.

"Papa said that when you have logged enough hours with Kids Dig It, you can apply to participate in an archaeological project of your choice. He also said that if we complete the assignments for the Panama dig, we should have quite a few credits. And those credits might be enough to get us a trip to see whatever interests us."

"We could all go to Peru to see the Nazca Lines," Rachel suggested.

"Or the Acropolis in Athens," Anna said dreamily.

"Or Stonehenge in England," I said.

"You know what would be neat?" Eric said, starting to cheer up. "If we could fly down and surprise Jerome in the desert. I'd love to search for dinosaur fossils with him some day."

Anna didn't know that Jerome was the old trapper who we had recently saved at Impact Lake, but Rachel and I nodded.

"So if your parents grant you permission to come along," Anna said, "you boys will join us?"

"Yes," I said, and then remembered my manners. "And thanks for offering to take us along."

"Yeah," Eric said. "Sorry I freaked out. I'm just not a big fan of extra-curricular homework."

"Huh?" Anna said. "What does that mean, Eric?"

"It means he's lazy," Rachel said. "Really, really lazy."

"There is a problem," Bruno said, returning to the table and sliding in next to Rachel. He looked even more agitated than he did in the kitchen.

"What's wrong, Papa?" Anna asked.

Bruno lowered his voice and whispered, "That was your Uncle Rudi on the phone."

Eric looked at me and then at Bruno. "So how is that a problem?"

"Rudi was on a satellite phone from the camp, and the connection was not very good, but he said that he has been arrested for stealing artifacts from the site."

"Oh, no!" Anna cried.

"Shhh," Bruno cautioned, glancing back at the house. "I do not want to alarm anyone."

We all knew he meant our parents, so we kept our voices low.

"I guess we won't be going to Panama now," Rachel said.

"Yeah," I said. "I suppose they'll shut down the whole dig until this is cleared up."

"No, no, no," Bruno said. "Rudi absolutely needs your help to clear his name. You must come to Panama—especially now."

"How the heck can we help?" Eric said.

"Yeah, maybe you should hire a private detective," I said. "We're just kids."

"But that's exactly your advantage! You can blend in with all the other children at the camp. You can listen to the rumours. You can observe and watch for anything suspicious. It is much easier for you four young people to gather information than it is for any adult. You are Rudi's best chance to have his name cleared."

"That sort of makes sense," I said. "But I still think he'd be better off with a lawyer."

"He has contacted a lawyer," Bruno said.

"Good," Rachel said.

Bruno shook his head. "Not really. In Panama the theft of antiquities is a serious offence, so he is being kept under house arrest—or tent arrest, I suppose—until the artifacts have been returned."

"And if they're not returned?" Eric asked. "What happens then?"

"Rudi will spend a long time in a jail."

"What did he steal, anyway?" Eric asked. "Sorry, what are they *claiming* he stole?"

"There was a disturbance in the line," Bruno said. "But I believe he said a skull—some sort of crystal skull."

"Cool," Eric said.

Rachel glared at her brother. "There's nothing cool about any of this."

Eric looked apologetically at Bruno and Anna, then said, "I mean, at least he's accused of stealing something interesting, not just a broken pot."

Rachel shook her head at Eric. "Don't worry," she said, patting Bruno's hand, "we'll help in any way we can."

"I know you will. But before you kids make a final decision about coming with us," Bruno lowered his voice even more, "I need to caution you about *three* more things."

"Don't tell me they only eat turnips in Panama," Eric said, trying to lighten the mood. "Because then I'm definitely not going."

"Hush," Rachel said. "This is serious."

Bruno looked at the house and then started again. "First, I have seen digital photos of some of the pottery pieces that were uncovered by the contractors. And one of the larger fragments was decorated with three pillars. In fact, they look identical to the stones here in Sultana, in your cemetery."

"So you're saying there might be similar astronomical markers in the area where the dig is?" I asked.

"Exactly," Bruno said. "I cannot think of any other explanation. These stone formations are located around the world, but I doubt other archaeologists appreciate the significance of the stones as a time travel portal. But given what happened here last month, I felt I should tell you children."

That wasn't going to stop us from wanting to help Rudi, and we told him so.

Bruno nodded his thanks. "Now, my second caution may sound like crazy talk, but ever since publishing papers on these petroforms, I have had the feeling that I am being watched. And now I am worried this whole incident with Rudi could get even more … even more *dicey*."

Eric's eyes widened. "So you think someone is spying on you?"

"Who?" I said, equally intrigued.

"It could only be one person," Bruno said. "His name is Mr. Anton Zola, and he's obsessed with ancient artifacts and time travel. Mr. Zola is one of the few people who has always believed my theory about the astronomical markers. He is so desperate to get his hands on my research, I think he even broke into my office. I don't have any proof, of course, but I am almost certain it was him."

"Can't you tell him to buzz off?" I said.

"It is not that simple," Bruno said. "He is a billionaire and he has a lot of resources at his disposal. He has people everywhere reporting back to him." He stopped talking and seemed to be deep in thought. "Actually, *that* would explain how—"

"I don't think any of that matters to me," Eric said, getting excited and cutting him off. "I'm going to be too busy playing Sherlock Holmes, trying to figure out who's stealing artifacts. And if I do happen to find those crazy stones, I'll just stay away from them—far away."

"Yeah," I said, "I still want to go. I want to help Rudi."

"Me too," Rachel said enthusiastically. "I want to keep Rudi out of jail. *And* I want to see the most famous shortcut in the world."

"What?" Eric said.

"The Panama Canal, dummy."

Before Bruno could tell us what the third thing was that he wanted to warn us about, the house door suddenly opened. Our parents came outside and walked over to the picnic table.

Dad stood beside the table smirking. "Okay, you can go," he said. "You've all demonstrated last week that you can be responsible, so for that reason we'll let you go to Panama with Dr. Wassler and Anna."

Bruno clapped his hands together. "That is tremendous," he beamed, slapping Eric on the back. "Now, is there perhaps a medical clinic near here? We must quickly make arrangements for your malaria shots."

"Our WHAT?!" Eric cried.

CHAPTER 2

PANAMA CITY, PANAMA

"RACHEL, CAN YOU carry my bag for me?" Eric said. "My arm's still really sore from all those needles."

"You only got one shot," Rachel reminded him, taking her bag from the airport shuttle van. "In fact, we *all* only got one shot." She headed toward the Panama City Marina and our waiting boat.

"Yeah," Eric shouted at her back, "but it felt like ten!" He looked at Anna and rubbed his shoulder where he got his malaria shot the day before. But she gave him no sympathy either.

"You should not have flexed your arm muscles when you received the needle," Anna said, repeating the nurse's instructions. "Then you would not be in pain now." Anna fished her bag out and followed Rachel to the boats.

"I wasn't flexing," Eric complained, "my arm is naturally muscular."

"That was pretty good acting," I said, when the girls were gone, "but it looks like you're going to have to carry your own bag."

Eric laughed. "Yeah, I didn't think they'd fall for it, but it was worth a try." He hoisted his backpack from the vehicle and slung it over his shoulder. "For a second there, I thought I had Rachel fooled. That would have been sweet."

Bruno paid the driver of our van and joined us. "Welcome to Panama, boys." He took off his suit jacket, rolled it into a ball, and shoved it inside his giant backpack. It was hot and super humid, and I didn't think we'd be seeing that jacket again.

After landing at the Panama City airport two hours earlier, we all piled into a van and headed straight for the waterfront. Bruno explained that the only way to get to the dig site was to hop on a boat and use the Panama Canal. That's why we were waiting around a marina with a hundred other tourists.

On the long flight, Bruno made at least a dozen phone calls, trying to get as much information as he could on the situation with Rudi. Whatever he found out seemed to help him relax, because he looked a lot less stressed out than when we left Sultana and a lot more optimistic that we could somehow help sort everything out. I wasn't nearly as hopeful as he was, but I sure wasn't going to tell him that. Even though we didn't discuss it, we were all trying extra hard to stay upbeat and positive for Bruno.

"Which boat is ours?" Anna asked her father when the three of us caught up to her and Rachel.

Bruno examined the seven water taxis tied to the docks. "Look for a vessel called the *Balboa*."

"That's cool," Eric said. "They named a boat after a boxer—Rocky Balboa."

"I doubt they were thinking of a Hollywood movie when they named it," Rachel said. "More likely, they named the boat after Vasco Nuñez de Balboa—one of Panama's first explorers."

We all looked at Rachel with open mouths. *How the heck did she know that?*

"My ebook reader," she said, answering our unspoken question. "I was reading all about Panama on the plane."

"There it is," Eric said, pointing at the second last boat.

Bruno studied the back of that vessel. "That is it," he agreed. "And it has been reserved for our use."

"The *Balboa* looks kind of big for five people," I said. It only had one level, or storey, or deck—or whatever it's called—but I was sure it could carry a hundred people.

Bruno shook his head. "No. I mean, it has been rented for the archaeologists to use for the duration of the dig. It is to ferry people and gear back and forth to the site. Other teams may be joining us shortly."

"Where exactly is the site, anyway?" Rachel asked.

"Yeah," Eric said, "is it far from here?"

"Let's get our gear on board first," Bruno replied, "and I will show you the map."

We wound our way through the throngs of tourists, all waiting to take a day trip through the canal with one of the many tour boat companies. When we got to the *Balboa* we waited next to the gangplank until the captain saw us. He waved a greeting from the open window of his cramped wheelhouse, but didn't bother coming out. The name painted on the door suggested he was Captain Cedric Pescada. He bellowed at a young man who was sleeping in the middle of a coiled rope as thick as my wrist. The deckhand sprang to attention and helped us stow our bags in the rear of the boat. His English was pretty good and he seemed friendly.

"I would like to ask the captain if we can leave immediately," Bruno said, "but I think it might be polite to wait an hour or so to see if any other teams show up."

We all wanted to get to the camp and begin sleuthing around as soon as possible, but it would seem odd if we demanded that a nearly empty boat leave immediately.

"Show them the canal," Anna said, "and Lake Gatun."

Bruno nodded. "Ahh, yes, the map."

The *Balboa*'s deck was covered with a canvas canopy that protected passengers from the tropical sun and rain. The sitting area was made up of row after row of plastic chairs fastened directly to the metal decking. Some of the rows had long, narrow tables in between so that people could eat or talk. We made ourselves comfortable around one of those tables.

The deckhand came over and identified himself as Elvis de Tortuga. He saw the corners of Eric's mouth twitch and quickly explained that his mother was a huge fan of Elvis Presley, the famous American singer. He asked Bruno if he could get anything for us, so Bruno gave him money to buy drinks and ice cream for everyone—*including* Elvis. His face lit up and he jumped into action. He leaped off the side of the boat and onto the dock without even bothering to use the ramp.

"I think Elvis likes ice cream even more than you do, Eric," Anna said.

"I didn't think that was possible," Rachel said, "but you could be right."

By the time Bruno found his map, Elvis was back with a bag full of water bottles and ice cream sandwiches. We all thanked him and he drifted away to enjoy his ice cream and another nap.

"Okay," Bruno said, pinning down the corners of the map with our water bottles. "This is Panama." He placed both palms on the map and smoothed the surface in every direction.

"It's not a very big country," I said.

"No, it isn't. On a clear day you can stand in the mountains and see both oceans—the Pacific and the Atlantic. It's quite remarkable, really."

"You've been here before?" Eric asked, licking ice cream from his knuckles.

"Yes, I did some research here five years ago..." He stopped and looked at Anna. "Or was it six?"

"It was six years ago, Papa."

"Oh," Bruno said. "Yes, I suppose it was."

"And this is the Panama Canal here?" Rachel said, pointing to the narrowest part of the country.

"*Ja*, yes," Bruno said. "*That* is the famous Panama Canal—a man-made wonder of our world and an amazing feat of engineering." He spoke with such admiration, we stayed quiet and stared at his finger as he traced the waterway. "It is seventy-seven kilometres long and has three sets of locks that use water from Lake Gatun to raise and lower ships," he continued. "And when we leave here, the boat will take us north through the first set of locks and then into the canal system—"

"North?" Eric interrupted. "Don't you mean east? Doesn't the Panama Canal connect the east and west—the Atlantic to the Pacific?"

Bruno took several bites of his ice cream. "Excellent observation, Eric, but, no." He twisted the map so that it was directly in front of Eric. "The country of Panama has a unique S-shape. The narrow strip of land where the canal is runs from the west to east, but the canal itself generally follows a north to south path. It confuses many travellers."

"Hmmm," Eric murmured.

"Show them where we are going," Anna said, keeping her dad on track.

"We are going... here." His finger jabbed a spot on the map. "To the south end of Lake Gatun."

"That's where they found the artifacts?" I asked.

Bruno nodded.

"Is that where Uncle Rudi is?" Anna asked.

He nodded again.

Eric cleared his throat. "And that's where they're rebuilding the locks?"

"Actually, there are no locks right there," Bruno said, "but this is an important section of the canal that must be widened and deepened."

A ship's foghorn suddenly boomed and we all turned to look out across the harbour.

"Holy smokes!" Eric cried. "Look at the size of that ship!"

Eric and I raced to the railing on the side of the *Balboa* to watch a giant container ship packed so high with colourful boxes, it was hard to understand how it stayed upright. Two tugboats helped guide the monstrous boat into the Canal Zone. The girls and Bruno joined us a few seconds later.

"Isn't that amazing, Rach?" Eric asked his sister.

"If a ship like that can fit through the canal," I said to Bruno, "why do they need to make it bigger?"

"Because there are many ships that are much, much larger," Bruno said.

"You gotta be kidding," Eric said. "You mean there are boats *bigger* than that?" He pointed at the hulking vessel as it slipped down the channel. It looked so close, I felt I could reach out and touch it, yet it was over a kilometre away.

"That ship," Bruno said, "is called a Panamax and—"

"How do you know that?" Rachel asked. "I still can't see the back of it, where the names are painted."

Bruno laughed. "No, Rachel. Panamax is not the name of the boat. It is what all the maximum size ships on the Panama Canal are called. A vessel bigger than that cannot use the canal because it just won't fit."

"So they're making the canal wider and deeper for those ships," I said.

"Yes." Bruno nodded and finished off his ice cream. "The supertankers, for example, have to travel all the way around South America right now. If they could use the canal they could shorten their journey by almost thirteen thousand kilometres."

"And save a ton of money on gas," I said.

"Wow!" Eric said. "This thing really is a shortcut."

"Told ya," Rachel said.

We watched from the railing as another ship—some sort of ore carrier—left the canal and headed out into the Pacific Ocean. Bruno explained that the canal had two lanes of locks so that ships could travel in both directions at the same time. I imagined it to be sort of like a water highway, which is exactly what it was starting to look like.

As soon as one boat vanished, another seemed to appear like magic. It was crazy. After twenty minutes of watching a variety of different ships come and go, we walked back to our table and sat around the map again.

"Now," Bruno said, "where was I?"

"Lake Gatun," Rachel said.

"Yes. When we leave here, we will head to the first set of locks at Miraflores." He began pointing at locations on the map. "Next we will use the Pedro Miguel Locks, and from there we will cruise through the man-made Gaillard Cut to Lake Gatun. We won't see the third or last set of locks at Gatun, because they are on the north end of the lake and we aren't going that far."

We all murmured that we understood.

"And the artifacts were found here," Bruno said, poking the map again, "and that is where the camp is."

"It looks kind of isolated," I said.

"It is," Bruno agreed. "Everything we need must be brought in to the camp by boats or barges using the canal."

No one said anything for a minute. We were all staring at the map and the tracts of jungle that surrounded Lake Gatun.

Bruno broke the silence and answered the question we were probably all thinking. "The archaeologists will be exploring a narrow strip of land, right between a dense rain forest and one of the busiest shipping lanes in the world. And the five of us will be looking for clues to try and figure out why Rudi is accused of theft."

"No problem," Eric said. "I just wish I had one of those goofy hats. I'd really feel like a detective with one of those hats that have the visor on the front and the back, and the side flaps that you tie up on top."

We laughed lightly at Eric's silliness, but we also knew we'd be racing against time to help Rudi. Bruno explained earlier that if Rudi didn't return the artifacts within three days, or confess where he hid them, the police would take him to Panama City and officially charge him. And since he didn't steal or hide anything, there was nothing he could do. The bottom line was, we had to hurry and figure out what was happening.

After two hours of patiently waiting for other team members to show, Bruno had enough and went to the wheelhouse to speak to the captain. I could have easily hung out in the shade for another hour watching the ship traffic, but Bruno was looking kind of restless and twitchy. I suspected he wanted to talk to his brother ASAP. And who could blame him? Plus, I'm sure he didn't want to have to pitch a tent in the jungle in the middle of the night with four kids. Can't blame him for that either. With my luck I'd set up our tent on a mound of poisonous ants, or next to a huge snake, or... Well, you get the idea.

I saw Captain Pescada nod at Bruno, and a few seconds later the engines rumbled to life beneath the deck.

"Here we go," Eric said.

Elvis was about to untie the ropes that held us in place, when we heard shouts from the dock.

"WAIT!" A voice called out. "Don't leave yet!"

A few seconds later, seven people jostled aboard the *Balboa*. They mumbled their thanks and appreciation to the captain as they settled themselves.

Bruno seemed to recognize one of the adults and walked over to embrace a tall, lanky man in his sixties who wore thick glasses. They hugged each other enthusiastically like long lost friends. The other grown-up—a much younger man—waited patiently for the reunion to end.

All five kids on the team waved hello to us, but only one came over to visit. The rest stretched out on the rows of empty seats and seemed to fall asleep.

"Wow, that was a close call," the boy said when he was next to our table. "But I'm sure happy we got here before the boat left. I'm Ben, by the way, Ben Boswick." He held out his hand and we all took turns shaking it.

I explained who we were and where we were from.

Ben nodded. "Our team is from the United States. I live in Houston, Texas, and those guys are from Seattle and New York."

"Your friends seem very tired," Anna said.

"Who?" Ben asked. "Oh, right. Actually, I only just met them at the Panama City airport. They seem like nice guys, but they're not my friends."

"But how come they're so sleepy?" Rachel asked.

"They had a much longer flight than I did. And they said they had a lot of stopovers and delays." Ben adjusted his glasses, looked over at his travelling companions, and laughed. "But I'm way too excited to sleep. Panama is awesome!" His Texan accent reminded me of cowboys in western movies.

"We can see that," Anna said pleasantly. "Why don't you sit with us and relax."

Ben grinned. He was about as tall as Eric and had the same blond hair. He took a deep breath and sat down beside Rachel and across from me. "Yeah, I guess I am pretty pumped," he admitted. "But I just can't wait to see those skulls!"

"What skulls?" Eric said.

Captain Pescada, who had been helping Elvis remove the gangplank, suddenly appeared next to our table. He opened his mouth to say something, but then changed his mind and went back to the wheelhouse. *That was weird,* I thought. The boat shuddered a few seconds later, and we began to move away from the docks.

"Are you guys kidding me?" Ben asked when the *Balboa* was out in the channel. "You didn't hear what they found?"

"No," Anna said, "we've been travelling too. What did they find?"

Ben leaned over the table and glanced around the nearly empty boat—like whatever he was about to say was a huge secret. "Crystal skulls," he whispered. "They discovered crystal skulls."

CHAPTER 3

"YOU'RE JOKING," ERIC blurted.

"What?" Ben frowned and looked slightly hurt. "No, I swear. I checked the Kids Dig It website a few days ago. They posted an announcement that huge pieces from a broken crystal skull—two skulls, actually—were found at the dig site. They were buried under the floor of an ancient house."

We all stared at Ben, not knowing what to say next. We were stunned that we had met someone who might have information on the items Rudi was accused of stealing. And we weren't even at the camp yet. But I suppose Ben thought we still didn't believe him.

He jumped up and said, "I'll show you guys the pictures. I printed them."

When Ben was out of earshot and rooting through his bag, I leaned over the table and whispered, "There's no way that's a coincidence. Those skulls he's talking about must be the same ones Rudi is accused of stealing."

Anna and Rachel nodded.

"This is our first big break in the case," Eric said. "We need to find out everything we can about those crystal skulls."

"Should we tell Ben what has happened with Uncle Rudi?" Anna asked.

"I think we can trust him," Rachel said. "He can't be involved in anything, because he wasn't there when the skull was found, or when it disappeared."

"The more important question is: will Ben believe us?" I pointed out.

"Will I believe what?" Ben asked. He was so quick to return to our table with the pictures, we didn't hear him approach. "Will I believe what?" he repeated.

So we decided we had to trust him and started telling him our story. We began by explaining who we were and who Bruno and Rudi were. And we ended by telling Ben how, for some reason, Rudi was locked up at the camp and accused of stealing pieces of crystal skulls.

Ben sat and considered what we said quietly. Listening to us take turns telling the story, I had to admit the whole thing sounded nutty. When we finished, a tense minute of silence followed. I was sure he was going to laugh at us or get up and leave, but instead he turned to Anna and said, "We have to figure out who framed your uncle."

We all sighed with relief. We now had another investigator on our team.

"So you believe us?" Rachel asked.

"Well, yeah. Why would anyone make up a story like that?"

"So what's the deal with the crystal skulls?" I asked. "Can you tell us what you know?"

"Are they like the ones in the movies?" Eric said.

Ben unfolded a crumpled piece of paper and tried to smooth it out with his hands. "This is what they found at Camp Gatun," he said. "And this must be what Rudi is accused of stealing."

"Whoa!" Eric said, staring at the colour printout of two skulls.

I leaned over and studied the paper. The page was spilt into two photographs. One picture was of three pieces of a crystal skull. The pieces were placed close together so that anyone could see they formed the original skull. The crystal skull in the second image was broken into seven pieces, but still, there was no doubt they could all be glued together to make another head.

Ben pointed at the paper. "Neither one of these skulls was completely finished. The website said that they think the artist was working on the final details when they broke, or cracked, or whatever happened."

"I always thought crystal skulls were just a myth," Anna said.

"Crystal skulls are real," Ben said, "but *ancient* crystal skulls are a myth."

"I don't get it," Eric said.

"I know, it's confusing," Ben admitted. "But if these artifacts are real, and if this"—he tapped the paper again—"is a genuine crystal skull, properly found and documented, that's a huge deal."

The four of us were quiet for a few minutes. It was pretty clear that Ben knew a lot about crystal skulls. I sat back and watched as the *Balboa* followed two other tour boats into the locks at Miraflores.

Finally, Rachel broke the silence. "But why—*why* is a crystal skull such an important find?"

Ben was so excited, I don't think he even realized our boat was about to be raised by the first set of locks. "Okay, where should I start?" He took a deep breath and looked around. "Hey! We're being lifted."

Anna and Rachel laughed, but Eric and I frowned, wanting to hear more about the skulls.

I looked behind me and saw that Bruno and the two other archaeologists were now talking excitedly around another table. He was probably filling them in on Rudi's predicament too. "Tell us more about the skulls," I said quietly.

"Well," Ben began, "the four most famous skulls are the Mitchell-Hedges Skull, the Smithsonian Skull, the British Museum Skull, and the Paris Museum Skull."

"And they're all *crystal* skulls?" Eric asked.

"Yeah," said Ben.

"You said 'most famous,'" Rachel said. "Does that mean there are even more skulls out there?"

"Oh, sure. There are at least another dozen in collections around the world." Ben thought for a moment. "There's the Komo Skull, the Howard Skull, the Tiger Lily Skull, the Quazi-Minta Skull, and... and... Well, believe me, there are a bunch of them out there."

"Whoa!" Eric said. "That's a lot of skulls."

We watched as the water finished flooding and raising our boat. The gates of the first lock opened and the captain moved the *Balboa* into the second lock, where the water would lift us another two metres.

"But why are a couple of broken skulls in Panama so important that someone would want to steal them?" Anna asked, getting back to Eric's original question. "Especially if there are so many other crystal skulls around?"

"Because they're all fake," Ben said. "None of them are ancient."

"Wait a second," I said. "What about the ones that you said are in museums? Those must be ancient."

Ben grinned. "Nope. They're as phony as an armadillo with antlers. And that's why crystal skulls are so amazing. Pretty much everyone now knows that crystal skulls aren't very old, but they look *soooo* cool they're kept on display in museums anyway. And they're even identified as fakes. Imagine that—a museum proudly displaying a hoax!"

Rachel, Eric, and I exchanged glances. The three of us knew all about making good fake artifacts, because it wasn't that long ago that we created our own ancient Egyptian tablet.

Ben's fascination with the skulls was contagious, and we continued firing questions at him.

"How do the museums know their skulls aren't ancient?" Rachel asked.

"No one knew for sure how old the skulls were until recently. Some people claimed the skulls were Incan or Mayan, some said they were ten thousand years old, and a few even insisted they were left here by aliens."

"Cool," Eric said.

"It wasn't until a few years ago," Ben went on, "that scientists had the technology to test the skulls to see how they were made and how ancient they really are. And guess what?"

"What?" I said.

"What?" Rachel asked.

"Yes?" Anna said.

"Enough with the suspense," Eric said. "Tell us already."

"Sorry," Ben said with laugh. "Well, they discovered that the skulls were probably made in Germany in the 1800s using some kind of rotary grinding tool. Ancient cultures didn't have rotary grinding tools, so the skulls had to be fakes."

"The 1800s sounds kind of old to me," Eric said.

Ben nodded. "But it's not when you consider most of the skulls were discovered during the 1800s."

"I get it," I said. "So they were actually freshly made when people claimed to have found them."

"Exactly," Ben said.

"How do you know all this?" Rachel asked.

Ben chuckled. "Because my dad was an engineer on the team that tested the skulls. And he told me everything."

Anna quickly processed Ben's information. "So if the crystal skulls found here in Panama are tested and proven to be authentic, they would be the first *real* skulls ever found."

"*Ever!*" Ben repeated. "It will be one of the greatest discoveries of the twenty-first century, and it will knock the socks off archaeologists around the world."

"And if we could help recover those missing skulls," Eric said, "we'd be part of history too."

"Yeah," Ben said. "Plus, it's possible there are still other skulls buried at the site."

I nodded. "That makes sense. If those broken skulls weren't totally finished, there might be unbroken, finished skulls out there somewhere."

"After we help clear Uncle Rudi," Anna said, "maybe we can look for them."

I never really thought too much about what we might find at the dig site until now. To be honest, I had been more excited about the trip to Panama than I was about digging around in the mud. But that was because I never imagined we might find a crystal skull. Sure, it would have been cool to unearth some pottery fragments and other stuff like that. *But a crystal skull?!*

When the *Balboa* left the second set of locks at Mira-flores, Captain Pescada hit the throttle, powering us north into the channel. Our tour boat was small and light, and thirty minutes later we were lifted by the Pedro Miguel Locks.

Over the next hour we passed many slow-moving barges, container ships, and oil tankers. There was no shortage of tug boats either. They flitted around like helpful bugs, always ready to assist larger ships with a quick nudge or tow. It was pretty neat to be cruising through a dense jungle on the most famous man-made river in the world.

"Hey!" Eric cried. "A cruise ship." He ran to the front of the boat with Ben and me hot on his heels. Anna and Rachel stayed at our table.

The *Balboa* pulled up behind the medium-sized passenger ship and waited patiently to pass her.

Eric read the name on the stern out loud: MS *Alexander Pushkin*.

"Sounds Russian," Ben said.

"It is," a new voice said.

We turned our heads and found Captain Pescada standing behind us. He was smoking the stump of a cigar and grinning. "Don't worry, gentlemen," he said, with a thick Spanish accent, "the *Balboa* will not crash into the poet ship. Elvis is quite capable."

I looked over the captain's shoulder and saw Elvis behind the controls in the wheelhouse. I didn't want to say anything, but Elvis actually looked *more* capable and *more* professional than Captain Pescada. I mean, sure, the captain was wearing some sort of official shirt, but it was covered with so much grease and dirt, it looked like he'd been sleeping on the engine room floor. The shirt was open down to his thick waist, where the last two buttons struggled to keep the thin fabric together.

"How do you know there are poets on that ship?" Ben asked.

Captain Pescada choked on his cigar and laughed. "No, no, no." Blue smoke pulsed from his mouth like the smokestack of an old train. "The *Pushkin* is one of five cruise ships the Russians built in the 1960s. Each ship was named after a Russian writer. Alexander Pushkin was a poet, you understand?"

We nodded and waited for him to leave. But he didn't. It was as if he wanted to say something but didn't know where to start. Meanwhile, Elvis took the *Balboa* alongside the cruise ship and slowly passed her. We waved back at dozens of passengers who were leaning on the railings of the decks that towered above us.

"How much longer until we get to Lake Gatun—to the camp?" I finally asked, trying to break an awkward silence.

"Two hours and ten minutes."

"Excellent," Ben said. "I can't wait to get there."

"You boys," Captain Pescada began. Then he paused and glanced around his boat. He saw Bruno and the two other leaders looking at him, so he smiled awkwardly and waved his soggy cigar. Lowering his voice, he started again. "You boys will be staying at the camp for the whole week?"

I nodded.

"As far as we know," Eric said.

"You may be tempted to wander from the camp," Captain Pescada said, "for some excitement, or fun, or adventure ... But I would not."

"Huh?" Eric said.

"I would not," the captain repeated.

"You would not?" I said.

"No." The captain took a final pull on his cigar and flicked it into the canal. "The Chocoan are not very friendly."

The three of us looked at each other. *What the heck was he babbling about?*

"What are they?" Ben asked. "Some kind of animal?"

Captain Pescada squinted at Ben, like Ben was pulling his leg. "No. The Chocoan live around Lake Gatun. They have been there for thousands of years and they are very protective of their territory—*especially* the jungle near your camp."

"All right," Ben said slowly.

"That's good to know," Eric added, "I guess."

"Um, yeah," I said. "Thanks."

He probably didn't think he was getting through to us, because he felt the urge to repeat his warning. "You will be safe at the camp with the other archaeologists, but do not wander into the forest—no matter what you see. The Chocoan are... well, they are different."

After the captain left us to resume control of the *Balboa*, we casually wandered back to the girls to tell them what he had said.

"That's really weird," Rachel said when we finished our story.

Anna nodded. "Yes, why should he be so concerned about us leaving the dig site?"

"Maybe there's something away from the dig site," I said, "that he doesn't want us to see."

"Yes," Eric said. "Something like the stolen skulls."

"Do you think he heard us talking about them?" Rachel asked. "Or about Rudi?"

"Could be," Ben said. "But the skull find isn't a secret. I saw it posted on the web... remember?"

"You know, we may also be letting our imaginations run away from us," Rachel suggested.

Eric disagreed. "No. I think we found our first suspect, and I think we need to keep an eye on the captain."

"He is one of the few people who have access to the camp," I said. "And it would be easy enough for him to swipe stuff from the dig site and move it up and down the canal. As a Panama Canal boat captain, he has the perfect cover to be an artifact smuggler."

"Keeping an eye on him and his boat should not be a problem," Anna said, "but what of his warning?"

"Let's just hope that we have no reason to leave the camp," Rachel said.

Eric and Ben nodded, and I quickly copied them. But as I studied their faces, I couldn't help wonder if they were thinking what I was thinking. *If we had to go into the jungle to help Rudi, we would.* I sure hoped we wouldn't have to, though.

"There it is!" Eric cried. His arm shot out and pointed at the shore.

"Yes," Bruno said. "That is the dig, Camp Gatun." He had joined us again and explained that the tall guy had been one of his advisers when he was working on his PhD. "What a small world it is," he said at least three times.

The *Balboa's* engines throttled down and the captain moved us toward land. He let the camp know of our arrival with three short blasts of his horn. And his arrival estimate was bang on, by the way. It took us exactly two hours and ten minutes to get to Camp Gatun from the point where we passed the MS *Alexander Pushkin*.

Our tiny boat suddenly came alive with activity. The change in the *Balboa's* rhythmic engine noise, followed by the sudden boom of the boat horn, immediately woke

49

Ben's sleepy teammates. They sat up, rubbed their eyes, and looked around for their chaperones. Elvis, meanwhile, was at the bow, ready to throw his rope to a local boy who raced down to the dock to meet us.

The dock began at the end of a trail that looked like it had been hastily carved into the jungle. There were no other boats tied to the dock, but I saw four canoes dragged high up on the muddy shore. Through the thick trees that lined the shore, I caught glimpses of Camp Gatun—tents, canopies, and other signs of life.

"They will be cutting back three hundred metres of forest to broaden the canal," Bruno explained as we waited for the *Balboa* to ease alongside the dock. "And then they will remove one hundred metres of shoreline."

"I can see why," Rachel said. "This looks like a tricky spot on the canal to navigate."

Just then, another container ship made the final turn on Lake Gatun, before entering the canal again. Two tugboats stirred up the water violently as they tried to help it round the corner. Finally, the tiny tugs had the ship lined up so that it could continue into the canal under its own power.

"When all this land has been removed," Bruno pointed at the jungle that was now Camp Gatun, "and the earth has been dredged, Panamax ships and supertankers will be able to easily use the canal."

"But they can't do any more digging or dredging until the archaeologists are satisfied," Rachel said, "right?"

"Correct. The contractors and the Canal Authority want work to continue as soon as possible, but they know it would be terrible to destroy a potentially important archaeological site without investigating it first." Bruno frowned at the dozens of orange bulldozers and excavators parked up on a ridge a kilometre away. "You will have to work fast to find out what happened to those skulls."

The captain cut the power all the way back, and the *Balboa* drifted toward the dock. When we were five metres away, Elvis heaved his rope at the boy on the makeshift wharf. The dock attendant caught the rope and began gathering it up as we floated toward him. When the boat squeezed against the tires that served as bumpers, Elvis casually stepped onto the dock and secured us to posts.

"Hello!" a female voice bellowed a few minutes later. "Welcome to Panama."

We had just finished offloading our gear and piling it on the dock. I looked up to find the source of the voice. It was a dark-haired lady in her fifties.

"And welcome to Camp Gatun," she said with a Spanish accent.

We all stopped what we were doing. Some of us mumbled "Hi" or "Thanks."

"My name is Sofia and I am the director of the Panamanian Heritage Department." She paused as if waiting for someone to accuse her of lying. No one challenged her so she continued. "I am also the site supervisor here at

51

Camp Gatun. If you need anything or have any concerns during your stay, please let me know."

We all nodded.

"I will show you where you will be staying, and then we will begin with a camp orientation tour."

That sounded reasonable, so we all nodded again.

Sofia asked our names as she waited for us to hoist up our backpacks and gear. When we looked ready, she led the twelve of us to the camp. I realized, from my burning leg muscles, that the camp area was way up on the side of a gently sloping hill. When Sofia stopped so we could catch our breath, I turned to look back at the waterway. Lake Gatun and its many islands spread out to the north as far as the horizon, while the man-made section of the canal—that was the Gaillard Cut—sliced south through the jungle toward the Pedro Miguel Locks.

"Check it out," Eric said, pointing at the canal. "Here comes the *Pushkin*."

A kilometre away, I saw the upper decks of the cruise ship gliding behind the rolling hills of the rain forest. "Cool," I said. "It looks like a jungle ghost ship."

Sofia was intercepted by two men who seemed to want to have a lengthy conversation about something. I had no idea what that something might be because they were speaking Spanish, but it gave us more time to inspect the area and watch the ship traffic. Eric and Ben took off their backpacks, quickly fished out their binoculars, and began tracking the *Pushkin*'s course. Rachel and Anna were ahead of us, talking quietly.

"Take a look," Ben said, passing me his powerful field glasses.

I watched the cruise ship for a few seconds and then looked to see if the *Balboa* was sticking around or heading back to Panama City. I grinned. The captain was sleeping in a folding lawn chair while Elvis and the dock attendant unloaded camp supplies. *What a guy!* A flash of sunlight beyond the *Balboa*—on the far shore—suddenly caught my eye. I tried to focus on the spot but lost it. *Oh, well. It was probably nothing.*

I took my time and again swept the shoreline on the other side of the canal with the binoculars. Jungle, jungle, and more jungle. Thick, green, dark, and dangerous—not very inviting at all. No houses, no people, and no reason for us to go there. Thank goodness.

Wait! I saw the flash of sunlight again.

Nothing reflects like ground glass. I was sure I'd read that somewhere. And I was sure that the lenses of binoculars were made of finely ground glass. *Was someone spying on us?* Whatever I saw was starting to make me curious.

I continued to scan the shore carefully for any sign of life. *Nothing but jungle.* A dugout canoe was dragged up on the mud between two giant trees, but there was no one in it. I heard Sofia say "*Gracias*" to the men, and our group started moving again, leaving Eric, Ben, and me alone. We would have to keep walking soon or risk being left behind.

"Hey, Eric," I said. "Check out the shore on the other side of the lake."

Eric swung his binoculars around. "What am I looking for?"

"Do you see the canoe?"

"Yup," Eric said. "What about it?"

"You see something shiny?" I asked.

"Nope."

"Too bad," I said. "I was sure I saw—"

"Hold it!" Eric cut me off. "See the big tree, the one beyond the canoe?"

I found the canoe again and carefully lifted the binoculars until I saw the giant tree.

"Do you see him?" Eric asked impatiently.

"Wait... Yeah, I do." There was a young man crouched behind the thick tree with his own set of binoculars.

"What the heck is he looking at?" Eric wondered out loud.

"Lemme see," Ben asked.

"OKAY, YOU GUYS!" Rachel shouted. "TIME TO GO!"

We ignored Rachel. Eric gave Ben his binoculars. Following Eric's instructions, he quickly found the guy we were watching.

"It looks like he's watching the *Balboa*," Ben said.

I knew we had to leave, but Ben and I continued to watch the stranger. Whatever we were seeing might be important—might be linked to Rudi and the missing artifacts.

But then the guy observing the boat swung his binoculars our way.

CHAPTER 4

SEEING THAT TWO people were now watching *him*, he ducked behind the big tree.

"YOU BOYS HAD BETTER HURRY!" Anna yelled, her voice already sounding distant.

Ben didn't respond to Anna, and instead cried, "Whoa! Did you see that?"

"What?" Eric demanded. "What happened?"

"He saw us!" I shouted. "And then he hid."

"You're kidding," Eric said.

"No." Ben backed me up. "It was really freaky. He was totally trying to hide from us."

I would have loved to stick around and figure out what that guy was up to, but right now we had bigger problems—we had to hurry and catch up to our group. And our group was almost out of sight. *Yikes!* It would be a terrible start if the camp director had to yell at us on the first day for getting lost and not following instructions.

Eric and Ben slipped on their packs, and I led the way through the half-cleared jungle. Before I'd even walked twenty steps, I was saturated with sweat. It was unbe-lievably humid and I felt like I was jogging in a sauna. It had been comfortable on the *Balboa* because we were all in the shade and there was a nice breeze from the boat's movement. But this was crazy hot.

We jogged along the path with our backpacks bounc-ing awkwardly behind us. The sweat pouring from my forehead stung my eyes and blurred my vision, and I had to really concentrate as I ran. There were stumps, roots, and people everywhere, and I was terrified I was going to trip on something or slam into someone.

Most of the people we passed seemed to be clus-tered together in archaeological teams comprised of kids and adults. And everyone seemed pretty focused on whatever project they were working on. I don't know why, but the adults we passed didn't look pleased with us. Maybe it was a rule that you couldn't run through an archaeological dig with a backpack when it was a million degrees outside. A few kids, however, did look up as we trundled by, and some even gave a friendly wave.

As we scurried across the jungle ridge, I saw a lot of collapsed, ancient brick structures. The site must have been a village at some point in the past. The forest had tried pretty hard to swallow up and hide the whole place, but there were still plenty of interesting ruins. I was look-ing forward to rooting around for an unbroken crystal skull after we got Rudi released.

Finally, we caught up to everyone near a cluster of large canvas tents. They looked like old army-style tents, with ten-foot posts in the middle and guide ropes stretched and pegged into the jungle floor. I felt like collapsing to the ground in a heap, but I didn't want to let on how far we'd lagged behind or how much we'd had to run to catch up.

Sofia stopped, turned around, and indicated with her hands that we should all form a semi-circle around her. "As you saw from the walk from the boat," she began, "the site covers a large area—approximately five hectares. The portion of archaeological interest is that section we passed through. Your living quarters and the rest of the camp are here behind me." She pointed over her shoulder with a thumb.

"I think I'm going to die," Eric whispered to Ben and me. His face looked like a ripe tomato—a wet, ripe tomato.

Ben nodded, but he was still huffing too much to talk. He dropped his backpack on the ground, found a water bottle, and poured it over his head.

Sofia frowned at the three of us.

"I saw a lot of big earth-moving equipment on the hill," the tall man from the other team said. "Did they get all that here using the canal?"

The camp director shook her head. "The first step in widening the canal here was building an access road through the mountainous jungle. That allowed the contractors to begin bringing in the large machinery you saw."

"So we could have driven here on a road?" one of the other boys asked, sounding annoyed. I guess he didn't like boat rides.

Sofia laughed. "You wouldn't want to use that road. It would take a whole day just to get here from Paraiso. The canal is much more efficient."

"Was it the road builders who discovered this site?" Rachel asked.

"No, it was one of the surveyors for the logging company. He had been marking the areas to be cleared when he began finding interesting artifacts among the old brick structures. We saw some of those structures on the way here.

"It looks like it was a village," someone said.

Sofia nodded. "Yes, perhaps a very *special* village. I will explain that later."

Murmurs of intrigue passed through the group.

Ben jabbed Eric and me with his elbows. "Crystal skulls," he said quietly. "That's why the place is special."

"Anyway," Sofia went on, "the surveyor suggested that logging be stopped until the area could be evaluated. And here you are—ready to evaluate." She laughed awkwardly at her own attempt to be funny, which prompted everyone to laugh awkwardly.

She explained a bunch of other stuff, but I found my brain was too excited—or maybe overheated—to stay focused. I kept thinking about Rudi, the crystal skulls, the captain, and the guy with the binoculars. It was certainly possible that we were imagining clues. But it was also possible there was a connection between the recently stolen crystal skulls, the captain, and whatever the person on the other side of the canal was up to. Eventually, I drifted back to the present and to whatever the camp director was saying.

"... So please ensure you dispose of all garbage properly and stay away from the compost area at the southwest end of camp. The food scraps there attract rodents, and those rodents attract the dangerous snakes I just mentioned."

Whoa!

I'd obviously missed something important and immediately wished I'd been paying more attention.

"WHAT?" Eric cried. I guess he wasn't listening either.

"SNAKES?" Ben shouted. "You got poisonous snakes here? What—like rattlers?"

Scratch that. *Three* of us weren't paying attention.

Sofia—and everyone else—looked at us like we were zombies with malaria. She ignored Ben's rattlesnake question and said, "I'll show you to your tents now, and you can all get settled in. Dinner is at 5:30, and at 6:30 each evening we have a presentation on the day's finds."

The first tent was assigned to us. Each tent had six beds, so to balance the teams Sofia asked if one of the American boys would be willing to join our group. Ben probably knew us better than he knew his own team, and he was quick to raise his hand. So our official team from

England now had members from Germany (Anna), Canada (Eric, Rachel, and me), and the United States (Ben), and no delegates from England. Anna pointed out how weird that was and we had a good laugh.

Bruno held open the tent door—actually just a big flap of canvas—and we all went inside what would be our home for the week. It was bright enough inside the tent because each wall had a large square screen window and an awning. The awnings—again, more flaps of green canvas—were also stretched out and staked to provide shade and deflect rain.

Bruno quickly claimed the bed closest to the door by throwing his bag on the cot. "I am going to find out where they're keeping Rudi," he announced, heading right back to the door. "Hopefully they will let me speak with him, and hopefully he can shed some light on this . . . this misunderstanding."

"Can we come with you, Papa?" Anna asked.

"Yeah," Eric said, "I wouldn't mind meeting him."

Bruno stopped at the tent flap and turned around. "I think it would be best—for now at least—if you children are not seen with Rudi. The other kids here may be more likely to share information with you if they believe you are not connected with the person accused of stealing artifacts. Do you understand?"

Anna looked pretty upset that she couldn't see her uncle, but she joined the rest of us and nodded. I mean, after all, it did make sense what her dad said.

Why would anyone want to tell us anything if they thought we were buddies with the culprit who stole the crystal skulls?

"I'll be back as soon as I can," Bruno said.

When he was gone, we all just stood around for a minute not saying anything.

Finally, Eric said, "I guess we have to sleep in these mini-tents, huh?" He ran his fingers over one of the fine white nets that hung over each cot.

Anna nodded. "Unless you want to get yellow fever, or West Nile virus, or—"

"Okay, okay," Eric held up his palm, "I get your point. They just look kind of creepy—like some sort of veil a monster would wear if it was getting married."

"I don't like the look of those either," I said, indicating the binders placed on each of our beds.

Ben lifted the binder from his cot and read the cover out loud. "*Kids Dig It—Participant Workbook*." He tossed the binder on the bed again without opening it.

Rachel and Anna claimed the two beds at the rear of the tent. A curtain could be stretched across the tent, separating our sleeping space from theirs.

"I think this is going to be a really interesting week," Ben said.

"Yeah," Eric agreed, "except for the homework stuff." He helped himself to a water bottle from a case of water bottles near the door.

Rachel glared at Ben and Eric for being insensitive.

Ben quickly turned to Anna and said, "Sorry. What I meant was it'll be interesting to work with you guys to get your uncle out of trouble."

"Yeah," Eric said, "that's what I meant too. But I do hate homework."

Not sure what we were supposed to do next, Ben, Rachel, Anna, and I all grabbed our own water bottles and sat down around the folding table near the entrance.

"What the heck took you guys so long back there, anyway?" Rachel asked Eric.

Eric sat down on a plastic chair. "We saw something *very* curious," he said.

"What was it?" Anna asked, looking up from the workbook she was flipping through.

So we told the girls all about the guy who was spying from the other side of the lake. Ben ended our summary by saying, "It was really weird how that dude dove for cover as soon as he spotted us watching him."

"That's exactly the way it looked to me too," I said. "He was crouched down one minute, spying on the dock or the boat or the camp. And the next minute—when he noticed us—he vanished."

"Perhaps he was watching the *Balboa*," Anna said, closing her workbook, "because he plans on stealing her."

"Could be," I said.

"Or maybe," Rachel suggested, "he stole the crystal skulls and now he's waiting to move them or hide them or sell them."

"Exactly," Ben said. "Anyone who knows anything about crystal skulls would know that an authentic skull is worth a ton of money—millions of dollars, maybe."

Eric grinned. "We now officially have two suspects—the captain and the guy we saw spying."

"We need to tell someone about that person." Rachel opened her water bottle and began drinking.

Eric and I just looked at each other. Ben didn't say anything either.

"Yes," Anna said. "If someone is planning to steal the boat or has the stolen artifacts, we must report it."

"We could," Eric said slowly. "Or..."

Rachel choked on her water. "What do you mean, 'We could'? We have to!"

Eric shook his head and lowered his voice. "We don't *have* to tell anyone anything—not right away, at least. Remember, our assignment is to gather information and that's what we're doing."

"Please tell me you're joking!" Rachel begged. "*Please*. After everything that's happened to us this summer, do you really want to run into more trouble?"

"What happened to you guys this summer?" Ben asked curiously.

"It's a long story," I said. "I'll tell you about it later."

A group of kids neared our tent, and we waited for them to disappear around the corner.

"Listen," Eric said quietly. "If we tell the camp director what we saw, the only thing that will happen is it will put the focus on us. Rudi's locked up, Bruno is his brother, and we're his delegation. How's that going to look when an hour after we arrive we claim we saw the skull thief across the canal? We'll look like dummies making outrageous accusations."

I nodded. "He's right. Even if Sofia believes us and sends someone to take a look . . . then what? They'd come back from the dock, say they saw *nothing*, and then accuse *us* of being troublemakers, or jokers, or worse."

"But what you saw cannot be ignored," Anna said. "What do you propose we do instead?"

I wasn't planning on proposing anything, so I didn't know what to say. But I lucked out because Bruno suddenly returned to report his findings.

"It seems," he began, "that after the crystal skulls vanished, someone came forward and identified Rudi as the thief."

"You mean, like an eyewitness?" Eric asked.

"Yes," he said. "One of the cooks said he saw Rudi leaving the artifact tent early yesterday morning—"

"They actually saw him?" I interrupted.

"No," Bruno said. "But he described the thief so exactly— size, height, hair colour—they assumed it was Rudi. He is the only person of that unique description in camp."

We didn't know what Rudi looked like, so Anna quickly explained that Rudi was a giant of a man.

"He sounds more like a bodybuilder than an archaeologist," Ben said.

"That might prove to be a useful clue," I said.

"In what way?" Eric asked.

Anna nodded. "If we find a man of similar description in or around Camp Gatun, that person may be the real thief."

Bruno began digging though his bag for a clean shirt. I think he was so distracted he wasn't really listening to us. "A lawyer will be arriving soon," he said. "I have asked for my meal to be brought to the tent where they are keeping Rudi. We will wait there for the lawyer. It may be a late night for me, so please do not wait up. Go to dinner in the big tent and then observe what you can observe."

We told him we would find out what we could.

Bruno stripped off his sweaty shirt and slipped on a dry shirt. "The police will be here tomorrow some time," he said, heading for the door again. "We must work fast, because we don't know what they'll do when they get here."

And like a flash, he was gone again.

Eric, Ben, and I quickly copied Bruno and took off our clammy, sweaty T-shirts and changed into clean T-shirts. Anna and Rachel drew the curtain divider thingy across the tent and changed as fast as us. Six minutes later we all headed to the dining tent.

"What a spread!" Ben said, taking his tray to the next station. "This is almost like the Mexican buffets we have back home."

"Yeah," Rachel agreed. "I think even Eric will approve of the food here."

I have to admit, I was a bit worried at first that we wouldn't like the food we'd be eating. But not anymore. As soon as we walked into the giant dining tent, I relaxed. The food smelled yummy, and the sixty or seventy other kids already eating seemed pretty happy with stuff piled high on their plates.

"It's nice to see familiar-looking grub," I said.

"No kidding," Eric said. "And even the stuff I've never seen before doesn't look revolting. Like this stew here." He pointed at a tray of veggies and meat mixed together.

"That's called *sancocho*," Ben said. "My mom makes it sometimes. It's great."

"Are those French fries over there?" Anna asked Ben.

"No," Ben said. "It's fried yucca root, but it does taste like a tropical French fry."

Satisfied with this explanation, Eric pinched a thick stack with the tongs and piled them on top of the *sancocho*.

The self-serve food line ended with a variety of colourful fruits. The girls stayed and added pineapple slices to their trays, but we ignored the fruit and went to find an empty table. I looked around the dining hall at all the people. Most of the kids looked like they were between twelve and sixteen years old. Anyone older than that was probably a real archaeologist or some kind of team leader or chaperone.

When we were all done eating we took our dirty dishes and sorted them into bins. But we didn't have to wash the dishes. *Yahoo for that!* Several Panamanian ladies hauled all the utensils into a dishwashing area. The kitchen and dishwashing area, I suddenly realized, were actually mobile kitchen trailers that were dragged right into the enormous tent.

We all sat back down and waited for the day's briefing—or was it a *de*briefing?

Anna noticed that I was still staring at the kitchen. "Papa said this camp was meant to be a work camp for the contractors," she said. "But when the artifacts were found, the men were sent back to work on the Miraflores Locks. It didn't make sense to dismantle the camp again, so the Canal Authority asked the archaeologists if they wanted to use the place while they were evaluating the site."

The sun had disappeared behind the jungle hills, and it was getting kind of dark in the tent. Someone switched on the lights and a big cheer went up. Like I said, everyone was in a good mood. Well, maybe everyone except Rudi. A few of the men helped rearrange tables, and then the older boys began carrying in boxes. A hush fell over the people in the tent. I guess they knew what was about to happen.

"Those must be the artifacts from the site," Rachel whispered.

"This is going to be sort of like a show and tell, huh?" Eric said.

Ben rubbed his hands together. "Maybe they found some more crystal skulls today. I have to pee, I'm so excited."

We all laughed.

Sofia made her way to the centre of the long row of tables. She remained standing as she looked over the people in the tent. A few of the kids were still chattering quietly, so Sofia put a finger to her lips and kept it there until all we could hear was the buzz of insects bouncing against the tent screens outside.

"Thank you," she finally said. "We have two new teams with us today, so please join me in welcoming the delegates from England and the United States to Camp Gatun." Sofia pointed at our table and at the table behind us, where the American boys sat.

Everyone applauded politely, so I doubt they knew we were pals with the artifact thief.

"Now," the camp director said, still looking at us. "I'd like each one of you stand up, state your name, and say something interesting about yourself."

"Oh, no," Eric groaned quietly, "I hate that kind of thing."

"Let's start with ... you," Sofia said.

And wouldn't you just know it—she picked me to go first.

I gulped and stood up. "Umm ... hi," I said. "My name is Cody, and I'm from Sultana. Sultana is in Manitoba—which is in Canada, by the way."

69

Sofia nodded. "Thank you, Cody. Please tell us something interesting about yourself."

I could have told her stuff that was so interesting it would have made her whole family faint. But I didn't think this was the time to explain my time travel adventures. So instead I said, "My friends and I recently explored a float plane training base from the Second World War. It was very interesting."

A murmur of approval rumbled through the tent. I guess anyone interested in history would think that was cool.

"Rats!" Eric griped. "That's what I was going to say."

I sat down quickly, relieved to get that over with. Fifteen minutes later we had all completed our introductions and mini-speeches. It was time to see some artifacts.

"We have made tremendous finds in the last three days," Sofia began. "Most notably, the discovery of crystal skull fragments by the Italian team."

A cheer went up in the far corner of the tent.

"Gee," Eric said, "I wonder where the Italian team is sitting."

"Hush," Rachel said.

"Maybe one of the Italians swiped the broken skulls," Eric said, "to take back to Athens."

"Athens is in Greece, you dummy," Rachel whispered.

"I don't care where they live," Eric fired back. "They're still suspects, as far as I'm concerned."

Sofia continued. "And we remain optimistic that those stolen exhibits will be returned before the authorities arrive."

"Someone stole the crystal skull you found?" one of the American boys asked.

"My apologies," she said. "I forgot that some of you weren't present for last night's discussion. Let me quickly review what we know so far about the site. The pottery fragments, projectile devices, and other trinkets found here at the dig confirm that this site is at least five hundred years old. We believe that there was once a community of twenty or thirty families—likely of Chocoan background—living here on the shores of Lake Gatun."

The camp director paused and looked at our table and the table where the American team sat as she spoke. A bunch of us nodded.

"And we found two skulls buried beneath the floor of one of the ancient homes. The skulls were broken and shattered along their internal crystalline fault lines. One skull was in three pieces, the other in seven. They appear to have cracked as the artisan worked on the final details." Sofia took a sip from a water bottle. "They were . . . they were both beautiful, and now they have both been stolen."

CHAPTER
5

"BUT *WHO* WOULD want busted skulls?" asked another voice behind me. "Especially if they weren't even finished."

"The fact that they *weren't* totally finished makes them even more valuable, in a way," Sofia said, sounding a bit more composed. "For almost two hundred years people wondered where crystal skulls came from—Mexico, Colombia, Cambodia... no one knew for certain. Finding two *unfinished* skulls, right here in Panama, might have proved that any real skulls originated in Central America. It would have been an amazing archaeological find."

Sofia looked like she didn't want to talk about the skulls anymore. She took a deep breath and began lifting the lids off of boxes and pulling out various objects. She explained what each find was and how it was made. Arrow-heads, bits of cookware, trinkets—she seemed to have a little bit of everything.

Ben kept craning, twisting, and fidgeting in his chair. He really wanted to know if any more skull fragments were discovered, and he was growing impatient with the tiny muddy objects we could barely see from where we were sitting. When Sofia *didn't* pull a skull from the last box, Ben snapped. He jumped up and raised his arm.

"Yes?" the camp director asked. "Ben, is it?"

Ben nodded. "So, I guess you didn't find any more crystal skulls today, huh?"

"No, we did not."

"Oh," Ben said. "But do you reckon there might be more out there?"

The tent grew eerily silent as we waited for the camp director's answer.

"Finding the pieces of two broken crystal skulls was like finding a needle in a haystack," she said, "or winning a lottery. Yes, there may be another crystal skull around here somewhere, but I think our chances of ever finding it are ... are miniscule."

One of the team leaders from across the room stood up and asked. "Do you think the missing artifacts have been smuggled out of the camp, or could they still be here somewhere?"

After a minute of contemplation, Sofia said, "The overland construction road is in such poor shape, I don't think anyone could have used it. So, yes, it is possible the pieces are still on site."

"Who would do such a thing, anyway?" someone yelled.

Sofia placed a finger to her lips again, but this time she had to keep it there a long time. Finally, everyone had calmed down enough for her to speak. "I have no idea, but because potentially priceless artifacts have gone missing, we have requested a full police investigation. They will hopefully arrive on one of the morning canal shuttles."

I watched her closely as she spoke, and it seemed like she was staring at our table a lot. I'm not sure if she knew that Bruno and her prime suspect, Rudi, were brothers, but if she believed Rudi was guilty, there was no way she was going to be helping us.

Eric elbowed me and said, "I think I'll add her to my list."

"Huh?" I said.

"My suspect list. She knows those broken skulls are worth a lot of dough, so maybe she swiped them. She has access to the whole camp... so you never know."

"Once the police arrive at Camp Gatun," Sofia said, now glaring at the five of us, "I will leave the matter to them."

"She can't possibly think Rudi stole those crystal skulls," Rachel said. "He's a respected scientist and famous archaeologist."

"*We* know that," I said, "and so does the camp director, but I suppose she had to believe an eyewitness—at least until someone figures out what really happened."

Twenty minutes had now passed since the camp director gave her report. We were back in our tent again and sitting around the table. The single bare light bulb hanging above us cast an eerie glow on our faces. Bruno was still with Rudi, and we were alone. As anxious as we were about clearing Rudi's name and finding the artifacts, we weren't sure where to begin or what to do next.

"I suppose we could go from tent to tent," Rachel suggested, "and talk to the other teams. You know, interview them and ask if they've seen anything suspicious."

"We've already seen lots of suspicious stuff," Eric said. "I say we start with that."

"Do you really want to follow around the Italian team," Rachel asked, "to see if they lead you to the skulls?"

Eric shrugged. "Why not? That's better than doing nothing."

"I wish we knew more about detective work," Anna said.

"A detective would probably begin with the prime suspect," Ben said. "The most suspicious person."

Eric said, "I can't think of anyone more suspicious than that guy hiding in the jungle spying on us."

Ben nodded.

"There's no harm in going down to the dock and seeing if he's still around," I said.

"Bruno did say we should gather information," Eric added. "And that's what we'd be doing."

Anna and Rachel were quiet for several minutes. All we could hear were the billions of jungle bugs making noise outside.

Ben finally shattered the silence. "It's not like we're going to arrest anyone or do anything dangerous. We'd just be snooping around."

"But how can we do that?" Anna asked. "It's far too dark to see anything outside."

Ben suddenly grinned mischievously. He looked outside the screened tent windows and lowered his voice. "Wait till you see my flashlight."

Rachel frowned and said, "Uhmm . . . I hate to tell you this, Ben, but we all have flashlights."

"Not like mine, you don't."

"Okay, but how's a flashlight going to help us find the thief or the skulls?" Rachel asked.

Ben's feelings didn't seem to be hurt by Rachel's comments, and he laughed easily. Still grinning, he stood up and walked over to his backpack. We waited for him to dig something out.

Ben returned to the table with an object in each hand. "Did I mention that my dad's an engineer?"

"Yeah," Eric said. "You told us on the boat."

"Oh, okay," Ben said. "Anyway, my dad asked me to test this stuff under what he called 'real life conditions.'" Ben placed his binoculars and his flashlight on the table next to Anna's student workbook.

The flashlight looked bigger than most flashlights, but it still looked like a flashlight. The binoculars I had already used. Sure, they were nicer than Eric's, and more powerful, but they weren't spectacular either.

Eric immediately picked up Ben's flashlight and turned on the switch. Nothing happened. "Jeez," Eric complained, flicking the switch off again. "It doesn't even work."

Ben stood up and pulled on the chain dangling from the light bulb above us. *Click.* The light went off, and our tent was thrown into darkness. Our eyes slowly adjusted to the tiny amount of light trickling in from the rest of the camp.

"Why did you do that?" Anna asked.

"So that I can demonstrate the NightHawk IR," Ben said.

"The *what*?" I asked.

"You'll see." We heard Ben fumble in the dark with his binoculars. He pushed them into my hands and said, "Take a look outside—outside the tent."

"Huh?" I said. "At what? It's too dark to see anything out there."

"Trust me," Ben said. "Look down the hill."

I pressed the binoculars to my eyes and aimed them into the night. *Nothing.* "I'm not getting the point in doing this," I said. "It's all black."

"What about now?" Ben asked. "See anything?"

"HOLY COW!" I cried. "I can see for hundreds of metres. The trees, the trails, the dig—it's all clear as day." I lowered the binoculars and looked around the tent. But nothing had changed. The lights were off, Ben's flashlight was off, and we were all still in the dark.

"That's impossible," Eric said, already reaching for the binoculars.

"No. I swear," I said. "I could see everything out there."

"Lemme try," Eric said.

I passed him the crazy binoculars and he looked around Camp Gatun.

"WOW!" Eric said. "These are amazing. I really can see everything. It's all kind of greenish, but it's super clear."

"So how do those things work?" I asked, indicating the binoculars now pressed against Eric's face. "Do they detect the heat given off by surfaces?"

"No, it's not a thermal image," Ben said. "The Night-Hawk flashlight is an infrared searchlight. It shines a powerful IR beam that can't be seen by humans at night—or during the day, for that matter. But with the special lenses built into these binoculars, you can see everything that you shine the spotlight on. In other words, you need both—the spotlight and the IR glasses."

Eric passed the binoculars to Rachel so she could have a turn.

"I have to admit," Rachel said, "these are super cool, Ben."

"Thanks," Ben said. "My dad didn't invent infrared searchlights—they've been around for years—but he did develop these binoculars."

When Anna was done testing the gadgets, Ben clicked on the light over the table again.

Eric snatched up the flashlight and turned it on and off a few times. "This is wild," he said. "It doesn't even look like it's on—even when it's on."

"Yeah," Ben said, "that's what makes it so much fun. We could light up half the jungle at night and see everything, and no one would know."

I nodded. "So we could actually sneak up on a bunch of thieves hiding out in the night, and they wouldn't have a clue we were there."

"And then," Eric said, getting excited, "we could walk right into that camp and take back those missing artifacts. We'd be heroes."

"Then they'd have to free Rudi," Ben added.

Anna said to Rachel. "If the person they saw on the other side of the canal really is somehow involved in the artifact thefts, he may still be there."

"And if he's still there," Eric said, "we need to find him *before* he vanishes with the skulls... forever."

Rachel sighed. "Okay, you can count me in. But I'm not agreeing to anything unless we have a plan—a *real* plan."

I nodded.

Eric shrugged. "Sure, whatever."

"So, what's the plan?" Rachel asked.

"Well what about this?" Ben said. "It's still pretty early right now—only about seven o'clock, I think—and we're allowed to do what we want until the nine o'clock curfew. So why don't we take the NightHawk, go down to the dock, and look around?"

"And then what?" Rachel asked.

Ben shrugged. "I guess that'll depend on what we see across the canal."

Rachel frowned and looked at Anna. "That's not much of a plan."

"You gotta be reasonable, Rach," Eric said. "The next phase of our catch-a-thief mission will depend on what happens during the first phase."

Rachel laughed. "You make it sound like we do this all the time."

"But you're still in, right?" I said. "Because we need you."

Rachel smiled at me.

"Then let's go." Eric said, slamming his binder shut and jumping up. He wobbled on his feet and grabbed the plastic chair for support.

"Hey," Rachel said, "are you all right? You look kind of green."

"Yeah," Eric said, "I think I just stood up too fast."

We stuffed Ben's NightHawk in Rachel's small backpack and left the tent. The area around the tent city was still pretty busy. We saw some kids kicking a soccer ball under a light, while others played board games or read inside their temporary homes. We ignored the activity and made our way into the darkness of the dig site. We didn't know if we were allowed to wander through the ancient village at night, so to play it safe we didn't turn on our normal flashlights until we were clear of all the tents.

At first we thought we could get away with only using my flashlight, but we kept stumbling and tripping on the trail, so Rachel pulled out her flashlight too. But even with two flashlights, it was still pretty tricky trying to navigate the windy jungle path.

"Ouch!" Eric cried. He had been making up the rear, and it sounded like he'd tripped and fallen.

"You okay?" I asked, swinging the beam of my light on him.

"Sort of," he said, still on his knees.

Rachel shone her light on his face. "Did you break something?" she asked. There was real concern in her voice.

"No." Eric got up slowly and brushed the jungle crud from his legs. "I just don't feel very good all of a sudden."

We studied Eric's face with our flashlights. *Whoa!* His lips were purple and his forehead was shiny with perspiration.

"You look terrible," Anna whispered.

"I think I may have eaten too much for supper," Eric joked weakly.

"That's very possible," I said. "I don't think those cooks have ever seen a person eat six enchiladas."

"Are you going to barf?" Rachel asked.

"I hope so. I think I would feel a lot better if I did."

"We have to get you back," Ben said. "We can ask the camp nurse to come by our tent to take a look at you."

"Not yet." Eric pushed Rachel's light away from his face. "I want to see what's happening on the other side."

"Don't be a dummy!" Rachel said. "If you faint down by the water, we don't want to carry your sweaty carcass all the way back to the tent."

"But I want—"

Anna cut him off. "I will take Eric back to the tent. You three go and see what you can see."

That settled it. Anna took Rachel's flashlight and led Eric back up to the tent city, and we continued toward the dock.

Ten minutes later Ben stopped and whispered, "Turn off your flashlight now. I'll use the IR light so that no one can see us coming from the *Balboa* or the dock."

"Good thinking," I said.

Rachel and I waited for Ben to turn on his invisible flashlight beam and his modified binoculars. He held the powerful spotlight in one hand, and with the other hand he pressed the binoculars up to his eyes. As soon as I turned my flashlight off, Rachel and I each placed a hand on Ben's shoulders. Ben led us slowly toward the dock. I couldn't see where my feet were walking, but after a few minutes I sensed we were getting close. A refreshing breeze off Lake Gatun began to hit us in the face and felt terrific.

"Hey," Rachel whispered, "there's a boat."

Through the trees we caught flashes of tiny running lights as another giant ship navigated the tricky turn into the canal.

Ben stopped and did a thorough sweep of the area with the NightHawk. His shoulders suddenly tensed under my hand. Rachel must have felt it too.

"What's wrong?" she asked.

"This is bizarre," Ben mumbled. "It just keeps getting weirder and weirder."

"What's so weird?" I asked. "What do you see?"

"Well," he said, "the good news is, there's no one on the dock."

"Okay," I said, "that's good."

"But the bad news is, the *Balboa* is now on the other side of the canal and tied to a tree—to the very same tree that guy was hiding behind."

CHAPTER
6

"SO ANNA WAS right," Rachel said. "That guy was waiting to steal the *Balboa*—and now he has her."

"We better go tell the camp director," I said.

Ben passed me the binoculars, but continued to aim the IR spotlight across the water. "You guys might wanna take a look first—*before* we report that the boat got pinched."

I took the binoculars from Ben and looked at the area he was illuminating with the NightHawk. All the *Balboa*'s lights were turned off, but she was clearly visible in the eerie green monochromatic display of the binoculars. "I don't see anything suspicious," I said slowly. "There's the boat... There's the big tree we saw this afternoon... and... Hey, wait a minute! There's Captain Pescada!"

"What?" Rachel said. "They took the captain hostage?"

"No, he's definitely not a prisoner." I gave Rachel the glasses. "He's over there with Elvis, and it looks like they're both chatting with the guy we saw hiding this afternoon."

Ben and I waited for Rachel's opinion.

"This is nuts," she said after a minute. "Now I can see the captain passing shovels over the side of the boat to a fourth person—maybe a girl."

"Maybe he's just delivering shovels to some locals," I suggested. "Maybe there's nothing sinister about any of this?"

"Not a chance," Ben said. "This is the Panama Canal, one of the busiest waterways in the world. There's no way he'd turn off all his lights and risk being hit by another ship, unless he's up to something shady."

"And what's with the shovels?" Rachel asked. "Who the heck needs to plant a garden or dig a flower bed in the jungle so urgently that someone has to deliver shovels in the dark? That just doesn't seem normal."

"Unless," Ben said, "they're in a hurry to *bury* and hide something."

Rachel passed the binoculars back to Ben. "Something like two recently stolen crystal skulls?" she said.

"That would totally explain why the captain warned us not to leave Camp Gatun," I said. "He probably overheard us talking about the skulls on the boat, and he didn't want us to stumble on their hiding spot."

"And if one of his partners stole the skulls," Rachel said, "it makes sense that Captain Pescada would be nervous about getting caught. Maybe their plan all along was to bury the artifacts until the heat from the cops went away."

"Exactly," Ben said. "They'd know the police would set up blockades. And any boat leaving Camp Gatun would be easy to check too. The guy we saw with the binoculars this afternoon was likely just waiting for delivery of the skulls, or the shovels, or both."

"Jeepers," I said. "The artifacts may have been on the boat with us this afternoon."

"Or," Ben said, "sitting right next to that guy we saw hiding by the tree."

"There's only one problem with our theory," Rachel said.

"What's that?" I asked.

"Neither one of those guys fits Rudi's description. The whole reason Rudi is in trouble is because someone said they saw a big man. Those guys don't look anything like Anna's uncle."

"Maybe the witness lied," Ben suggested, "because he was in on the heist."

"Hmmm," Rachel mumbled. "I . . . suppose."

"I think we can move on to phase two," Ben said.

"And what's that?" Rachel said.

"I think we should go over there and see where they're burying those broken skulls," Ben said. "And that's all we do. We'll watch them with the IR light, memorize the spot, and return to camp. We'd be back here again in thirty minutes."

"Perfect," Rachel said.

"Really?" Ben said.

"Huh?" I said, equally surprised at her willingness.

"Well, duh?" Rachel said. "It's the only plan that makes sense. Those guys over there are about to bury priceless artifacts. We don't have time to go back to try and convince people we aren't fibbing. And even if the camp director believed us and called the police, they wouldn't get here until tomorrow. By then, those guys will have slipped away into the jungle. And Rudi will still be their number one suspect."

"Okay," I said, "we better hurry. Let's take one of those camp canoes we saw dragged up on the shore. If we're lucky, there'll be paddles around somewhere too."

Ben used his night vision gear to scout the best route to the canoes. Then, with our hands on his shoulders again, we followed him down to the water. Rachel and I flipped the first boat, while Ben hauled out two paddles and two life jackets wedged beneath. We borrowed a third paddle and third life vest from the next boat and tossed it in our canoe.

There were no stars or moon visible because thick clouds hid the sky. But our eyes had grown used to the darkness, and we were just able to see the water and jungle around us. We slid the canoe down the muddy bank, pushed it in the water, and climbed into the wobbly boat. The forest across the water formed a dark smear on the horizon, and we aimed our canoe into that direction.

After a minute of paddling, I heard Ben whisper from the front of the boat. "Do you guys see that navigational buoy, way over there on the left?"

"Yeah," Rachel said.

I squinted north into the blackness. At first I didn't see anything, but then, a few seconds later I spotted the flashing light that guided ships from Lake Gatun into the Gaillard Cut. "I see it," I said.

"We shouldn't get lost or disoriented," Ben said, "as long as we keep that buoy on the left side of the canoe."

I looked around for any other landmarks or buoys that might help us. "Hey," I whispered, "look behind us—at the jungle. You can see the lights from Camp Gatun reflecting against the low clouds."

"Excellent," Ben said. "That'll keep us oriented on the way back."

We stroked our way across the canal, trying hard not to splash the water with our paddles.

"At least there are no more giant ships around," I said to Rachel. She was sitting in the middle of the boat.

"Yeah," she said softly, "so far so good."

We planned on using the NightHawk again when we got closer to the *Balboa*, but for now our goal was to make it across the canal before a freighter slammed into us. I grinned because our plan was coming together nicely.

And then it started to rain.

I had never seen anything like it in my life. Water poured down so hard I couldn't see Ben—and he was only two metres away. Seriously! That was how fast and heavy the rain came down.

Ben said something over his shoulder, but I couldn't make out a word.

"WHAT?" I shouted.

"HE WANTS TO KNOW," Rachel yelled, "IF WE SHOULD GO BACK."

I shook my head and hollered, "NO!" I figured we were past the point of no return—halfway across the canal—so we may as well plow ahead.

We began paddling furiously. I knew from Boy Scouts that the canoe wouldn't sink, even if it filled right up with water. The problem was, as it filled—and it was doing that quickly—it was becoming harder and harder to paddle.

The minutes passed and the rain didn't let up. I began to panic. *What if our canoe was going in the wrong direction? What if a container ship was barrelling down on us?* We wouldn't even see a boat until it slammed into us.

Without warning, the canoe stopped dead and we all lurched forward. I had been in the middle of a powerful paddle stroke and the momentum threw me into Rachel. I knocked her from her seat, and we both splashed to the floor of the canoe.

"Sorry," I whispered, scrambling to get off her.

"Better you hit me," she said, "than the propeller from some giant boat."

"We made it," Ben's voice filtered through the rain. "We're on the other side."

The three of us tried to drag the canoe onto shore, but it wouldn't budge. It had way too much water in it. I was soaked anyway, so I slogged my way into the lake up to my waist. We rolled the canoe over while it was still in the lake and then lifted it from the water. Slipping and sliding we wrestled with the canoe and hauled it on the bank.

After we stowed the life jackets and paddles under the canoe, we fought our way through the brush and into the jungle. Ben found a tree with enormous leaves that seemed to direct the rain away from the trunk. Rachel and I joined him around the base.

"I think the rain is letting up a bit," Rachel said.

"Good," Ben said. "We have to wait for it to stop, if we want to use the night vision gear. It can't see through rain."

"Then we better wait right here," I said. "I have no idea if we hit the shore south of the *Balboa* or north of the *Balboa*. If we leave here now and walk even five metres, we're going to be lost forever."

Several minutes passed, and then as suddenly as it began, the rain stopped. The jungle dripped noisily, but we all agreed that the downpour had ended.

"Well," I said, "should we go back down to the lake and see where the heck we are?"

We found our canoe easily and studied the lakeshore. The buoy was off to the right—exactly where it was supposed to be—and the glow of Camp Gatun cast a friendly beacon across the dark water and to the southwest.

"Perfect," I whispered, "now we just have to find—"

A hand suddenly clamped over my mouth.

"Shhh," Rachel hissed in my ear. "Look to your right."

I spun my head to the right. Ten metres away there was an orange glow. It wasn't much brighter than a single bulb on a Christmas tree, and it seemed to pulse and fade. *Huh*? I wondered. *What was that?*

"It's the *Balboa!*" Ben whispered, reading my mind. "I think she's right over there!"

"But what was that light?" I asked quietly.

"Gimme a sec," Ben said.

I heard him fumble in Rachel's bag for the infrared spotlight, and a few seconds later the binoculars came alive with a soft electronic buzz. Rachel and I waited for his report.

"It's the captain," Ben whispered. "He's smoking a cigar under the canopy. He's looking this way, but I don't think he can see us. Keep still."

We remained frozen until he gave us the *all clear.*

"Okay," Ben said after a minute, "he's heading off to the wheelhouse. We can go after those guys in the jungle now."

It was comforting to know exactly where we were again. All we had to do now was head straight back into the forest and slowly work our way north. If we were lucky, and if the thieves were lazy, they wouldn't bury the skulls too far from shore.

Rachel had one hand on Ben's shoulder again, and I had a hand on Rachel's shoulder. And together, in single file, we began searching the thick jungle for the skull thieves. It only took about ten minutes for Ben to stop and freeze.

"I think they're up ahead," Ben whispered. "I saw movement."

"Hey," Rachel said, "I think I can see light over there— from a lantern or a flashlight."

"Yeah," I said quietly, "I see it too. There's a glow in the trees, about fifty paces ahead."

Ben lowered the binoculars, and we all crouched behind a thick tree. "Should I see how close I can get?" he asked. "You know, to see what's happening?"

"No way," Rachel said quickly. "I don't think we should separate, even if it is a bit awkward shuffling around the forest like this."

"I agree," I said.

"Good," Ben said, sounding relieved.

"I need to stop for a moment," Rachel whispered. "I think something scratched my leg or... or something. Can you please take a look?"

Ben played with the night vision glasses and adjusted them so he could see up close. A few seconds later I heard Ben moan and take a bunch of short breaths. It sounded like he was about to hyperventilate.

"Ben! What's wrong?" I asked. "Are you okay?"

"Don't freak out, guys," Ben said, "but—"

"But what?" Rachel demanded. "Tell me what you see." She sounded like she was about to freak out too.

"We're all covered in leeches!" Ben said. "Our legs, our arms, our necks... we're totally covered with them!"

"How?" I mumbled, dumbfounded. "We... we weren't even swimming." I felt like screaming and racing back to the canoe, but I knew that would be a big mistake. I took a few deep breaths and tried to control the terror I felt.

"It has to be the trees," Ben said. "The trees in the jungle must be dripping with them, and they're falling on us as we go by."

"Disgusting!" Rachel whimpered. "Get them off!"

"With what?" Ben said. "Aren't you supposed to use salt or a burning match?"

"No," I said firmly. "Just pull them off slowly and flick them away. That's what we were told to do in Boy Scouts."

Rachel sounded horrified. "Really? That'll work?"

I tried to control my voice so Rachel wouldn't freak out. "Yeah, you're actually *not* supposed to use salt or burn them. If you dump salt on a leech, it'll puke. And then you could get an infection."

"Gross!" she said.

Ben began pulling the slimy leeches from Rachel's legs. "I think I need help, Cody. There's too many."

Rachel groaned.

"I think we're far enough away," I said, "and well enough hidden, that I can use the small flashlight."

"Do it!" Rachel ordered. "Please hurry."

I found my Mini Maglite, wrapped the bottom of my T-shirt over the bulb, and turned it on. The glow was just enough for me to help Ben rip the pesky pests from Rachel's neck and arms. At first, I was disgusted by the slimy, boneless feel of the parasites, but there were so many, I quickly got used to it. I noticed that Rachel's leech wounds continued to ooze red—a mixture of blood, sweat and rain—long after I removed the bugs. But I didn't think this was the right time to tell her about the anticoagulant that leeches inject to better suck out blood. I only hoped we would still have enough blood left in us to make it back to Camp Gatun.

Rachel grabbed my light. "We'll do you next."

I had ripped so many leeches off of Rachel, they now no longer creeped me out. And even though I couldn't see anything, I tried to help out by yanking the ones I could feel.

When we finished picking Ben clean and were satisfied that we hadn't missed any, we covered our bodies in bug repellant. It stung like crazy on the leech wounds, and we didn't know if the DEET would even work to keep them away, but it was worth a try.

"Okay," I said, "let's go and see what we they're up to."

"Yeah," Ben agreed, "we gotta get moving—it's getting late."

The glow from the lights of the skull thieves acted as a beacon, but we still used the NightHawk to find the best route through the jungle. It would have been a shame to get caught now because we carelessly stumbled on a root and made a bunch of noise. Prowling ever closer, we followed Ben as he wound his way around trees and logs and bushes. The noise from the dripping canopy above us, and the soaked ground below our feet, helped disguise our approach.

Suddenly, I felt Rachel tug on Ben's shoulder.

Ben stopped and crouched behind a rotting log.

"I think this is close enough," Rachel whispered.

Ben passed Rachel the night vision binoculars, but we were so close now, we didn't even need them. Ten metres in front of us were three people—Elvis from the *Balboa*, a girl of about seventeen, and a man in his twenties. They were standing in a small circle and leaning on their shovels. A battery-powered camping lantern sat on the ground near their feet.

I ducked below the dead tree and whispered. "Okay, let's head back. We found our thieves and we know where they're burying the skulls."

"I'm not so sure anymore," Ben said. He was still pointing the infrared spotlight over the log and toward the thieves.

"What do you mean?" I said.

"Something doesn't make sense," Rachel said, handing me the binoculars. "Take a look for yourself."

I focused the binoculars and let my eyes adjust to the crazy green image. Elvis and the two strangers were standing in a tight clearing and discussing something quietly. The girl seemed frustrated with the hole they had just dug and began pointing at other spots in the forest around them.

I popped below the dead tree again. "I don't see any artifacts," I said. "But it looks like they're about to bury *something*."

"You better take another look," Ben suggested.

"Yeah," Rachel said, "look behind them a bit—on that higher ground."

I stuck my head up again and re-examined the area.

Huh?!

Now I knew what Ben and Rachel meant. *Something definitely wasn't right.* There wasn't just one hole. The entire area was peppered with holes—dozens and dozens of holes.

CHAPTER 7

I DROPPED BELOW the log. "Why would they did so many holes?"

"Exactly," Ben said. "It's bizarre. A hole is a hole. There's no need to dig a perfect pit to hide some stolen skulls. Any depression in the ground would do."

"And they couldn't possibly have dug all those holes tonight," Rachel said. "There must be a hundred little mounds out there."

"That's for sure," Ben said. "It looks like a thousand gophers live on the side of that hill."

"Let's get out of here," I said. "This is weird."

CLANG!

We all froze.

"What was that?" Rachel said.

"It sounded," Ben said, "like someone got bashed on the head with a shovel."

We lifted our heads above the log to see what was happening. The three thieves had moved up the hill ten metres and were now standing around a stone and arguing about something. The girl took her shovel and whacked a boulder. *CLANG!* She seemed really frustrated.

"I wonder what she's all fired up about?" Ben mumbled.

I still had the night vision binoculars in my hand, so I pressed them against my eyes for a better look. "Hey," I whispered to Ben, "light that area up—the area where they're standing."

"No problem." Ben swung his spotlight up the slope and penetrated the night with a blast of infrared light.

"No way!" I said. "I don't believe it!"

"What now?" Rachel demanded.

"Rachel, it's a pillar! They're standing around a petro-form. And it looks exactly like the stones in Sultana—in the graveyard."

"You've seen a stone like that before?" Ben asked.

I ignored Ben's question, passed the glasses to Rachel, and said, "Here, take a look."

"Anna's dad said the same astronomical markers might be somewhere in Panama," Rachel whispered, "but I sure never thought we'd find them here."

"What's the big deal about some stones in the jungle?" Ben asked, confused.

"We'll tell you about them when we're at camp again," I said. "Which reminds me—we better go back before we get in trouble."

"But there are only two," Rachel said, still leaning over the log and examining the area.

"Two people?" I asked.

"No," she clarified. "Two *pillars*. I can't see the third stone marker."

"Maybe it fell over," I said. "Come on, Rachel, we gotta leave."

Ben let me use the binoculars to guide us back to the shore and the canoe. When I saw that our boat was still where we'd left it—*thank goodness*—I turned the binoculars off and let them dangle around my neck. Ben flicked off his spotlight and we cautiously fought our way through the thick shrubs along the shore.

I suspected we were all covered with leeches again, but we would have to deal with them on the other side of the canal. We couldn't waste time removing them now, even though I knew they were slowly sucking our blood.

Rachel and I flipped the canoe quietly. I grabbed the back and was about to slide it into the water, when Rachel pulled on my elbow. "Take one more look around with the NightHawk," she said, her hands cupped around my ear. "Make sure Captain Pescada isn't looking this way."

I nodded. I'd almost forgotten that we came ashore a mere stone's throw from the *Balboa*.

"I'll get Ben to shine the spotlight on the boat," Rachel whispered.

Again I nodded.

I turned on the infrared binoculars and pressed them against my eyes. Ben was on the other end of the canoe, and I waited for Rachel to tell him to turn on his powerful light.

But the *Balboa* was already bathed in monochromatic green.

What?!

It took me several seconds to comprehend what I was seeing. And then I reacted... and I reacted fast. I leapt over the canoe and tackled a dark shadow—a shadow I hoped was Ben.

"Ugh." Ben groaned and toppled onto the muddy shore. "What are you doing?"

"Don't turn on your light," I whispered urgently. "Keep it off!"

"Why?" Ben asked. "No one can see it."

"No, no." I rolled off of him. "We can't use it, because there's someone else out there using one right now. I saw their light with the binoculars. If you turn on the NightHawk, they'll know we're here—they'll spot our IR light."

Rachel crouched down behind the canoe with us. "You're kidding," she said. "You mean there's someone spying on us?"

I passed Ben the special binoculars so he could see for himself. "Well, I don't know if they're watching us," I said, "but someone's definitely watching the *Balboa*."

"We should be okay," Ben said, after a minute. "It looks like the spotlight is coming from out on Lake Gatun, on the other side of the *Balboa*. So there's no way anyone could see us hiding here."

"It could be the canal police," I said. "Maybe they have a patrol boat out there somewhere."

"That's true," Ben said. "They may just be wondering why the *Balboa* is tied to a tree in the middle of nowhere."

"But why use night vision gadgets?" Rachel said. "Why not just turn on a giant spotlight and pull right up to the boat?"

Ben and I both mumbled that we didn't know.

"Captain Pescada must have gone into the jungle," I said, "because I never saw him on the boat."

"Good," Ben said.

"So as soon as *whoever* is out there turns off their IR spotlight," I said, "we can head across the canal again."

"We can use the light from Camp Gatun to guide us," Rachel said. "If we paddle to the right of those lights on the hill, that'll get us pretty close to the dock."

We waited nervously for the huge infrared beam to turn off. But it didn't. Ben and I took turns with the binoculars, watching the light sweeping the jungle and the shore around the *Balboa*. Finally, whoever was out there spying had had enough.

"Thank goodness," I said, passing Ben the binoculars. "The infrared is gone."

"Should we wait a bit?" Ben asked. "In case it's a trick?"

"I think we have to risk it and go," I said, glancing at the luminous dial of my watch. "It's getting close to nine o'clock, and we can't wait around any longer."

We slipped the canoe into the water and paddled silently across the canal. I sat at the back again and tried to aim our boat north of the tent city lights, where I guessed the dock was.

"See if anyone is tracking us," Rachel said, when we were halfway across.

Rachel and I continued to paddle while Ben scanned the area with the binoculars.

"Nothing," Ben said a few seconds later. "It's all black out there. I think we're in the clear."

I suddenly had an idea. "Hey, Ben, keep looking through the binoculars. I'm going to do a quick sweep with the infrared spotlight, starting behind me by the *Balboa* and ending somewhere near the dock."

"Okay," Ben said, "I'm ready."

I flicked on the infrared spotlight and slowly panned across the water from the east to the west.

"GOTCHA!" Ben said, excitedly.

I immediately turned off the IR light.

"You saw something?" Rachel said.

"You bet I did," Ben said. "There's a yacht—a really sleek yacht—hiding just behind the point. All its lights are off and I couldn't see anyone on the deck, but I'd bet anything that boat was the source of the infrared light."

"Hmmm," I said, paddling again. "Do you think it was there before—like *before* we left the dock?"

"Could be," Ben replied. "That boat is tucked in pretty good behind that spit of land. And I don't think we could have seen it from our side—not even from the end of the dock."

"I sure hope they didn't see us sneak across in the dark," I said.

We slid onto the muddy shore of the west bank only a few metres from where we'd left. Quickly, we dragged the canoe up the slope and in the position we'd found it. Rachel and I pulled out our flashlights, and we all began trotting through the dig site and back up the hill. We knew that we risked being caught with the lights on, but we were running out of time. It was almost nine o'clock.

Outside our tent, at the start of the tent city, we saw Anna pacing back and forth. She saw our lights approaching, flicked on her own flashlight, and ran down the trail to greet us.

Anna stopped dead in her tracks. "Oh, my God!" she cried, sounding like she was scared of us. "What happened to you?"

I looked at Rachel, because that was where Anna's flashlight was pointed. "Whoa!" I said, shining my light at Rachel and then Ben. "We gotta get cleaned up before someone sees us."

"*Cleaned up*?" Anna whimpered, still sounding like she was in shock. "You three look like monsters."

We examined each other with our lights and quickly removed the dozens of leeches that still clung to our flesh. Anna stepped back, horrified at our grizzly appearance and grossed out by the blood-sucking bugs.

When we'd flicked away the last parasite, Anna said, "I can't believe you still have blood left."

"How's Eric?" Rachel asked.

"He is okay now. He threw up twice and felt awful, but now he is sleeping. The nurse gave him something to settle his stomach."

"Does your dad know we took off?" Ben asked.

Anna nodded. "He returned briefly to fetch his notebook. I told him you three went to interview Captain Pescada. He believed me but will know I was lying if he sees you like this."

"Yeah," I said, "this looks really bad." I turned to Anna. "Can you get some clean clothes from our bags and go to the shower buildings? We'll sneak around the back of the tents—hopefully no one will see us—and meet you there. If we're lucky we can get washed up before anyone discovers us like this."

Asking questions and talking to the other kids was one thing, but prowling around the jungle, on the other side of the canal, in the dark . . . well, that was something entirely different. Bruno may not think that was valuable use of our time.

We wound our way south along the perimeter of Camp Gatun and waited for Anna in the shadows. Minutes later she showed up carrying her toothbrush in one hand and a plastic bag in the other. One of the other team leaders stopped to say hello to her. We heard her say that she forgot to brush her teeth and needed to hurry. The man said goodnight and kept walking.

Anna found us and passed out clean T-shirts and shorts, soap, and towels. "We will see you back at the tent," she said to Ben and me. She grabbed Rachel's hand and pulled her toward the girls' shower building.

Ben and I took off into the boys' shower. The two long trailers that served as shower buildings were the only structures other than the kitchen that weren't tents. And we were lucky—our trailer was totally empty. We each dove into a shower stall and did our best to wash away the dirt from our jungle adventure.

I found three more leeches—one under an arm pit (gross!), one behind a knee, and one on my neck. I dropped them on the floor and watched the water swirl them down the drain. *Good riddance.* Some of my leech wounds were still oozing a bit, but otherwise I think I looked presentable.

"Disgusting!" Ben shouted over the shower divider. "I found five more leeches."

"Put me down for three," I yelled back.

We both popped out of our change cubicles at the same time and left the trailer. Weaving our way through Camp Gatun, we walked briskly back to our tent. Eric was snoring softly, but otherwise our sleeping quarters were empty. *Whew, we made it.* We had just finished stashing our filthy clothes under our cots when Bruno walked in.

"Did you boys find out anything interesting tonight?" he asked, sounding distracted. I think his mind was still focused on his brother.

I wasn't sure how much to tell him, and I heard myself saying "Ummm."

Ben saved me by changing the subject. "Has Rudi's lawyer arrived yet?"

"Yes," Bruno said, "but things don't look good right now. The lawyer interviewed the witness who said he saw Rudi leaving the artifact tent, and the description fits Rudi's. You did not happen to see another giant man around?"

We both shook our heads.

Bruno drank some water from his bottle and said, "The lawyer believes this may take a long time to resolve if the skulls are not found. If only we could find them."

Ben and I didn't say anything.

Bruno shook his head, like he was trying to snap out of a daydream. "How's Eric doing, anyway?"

"A lot better," Ben said.

"The girls aren't here?" he said.

"They went to brush their teeth," I said quickly.

Bruno frowned. "Huh, I thought Anna did that earlier."

"Anna went along to keep Rachel company," I added quickly, in case Bruno was getting suspicious.

"Ah, yes," he said. "Of course."

Three minutes later, the nine o'clock curfew bell sounded, indicating everyone had to be back in their tents. Rachel and Anna walked in as the ringing finished.

I shook my head and sighed. What a night!

GONG. GONG. GONG.

A bell sounded somewhere in Camp Gatun and I opened my eyes and looked at my wrist watch. It was 7:30 AM.

"Okay, kids," Bruno said, tying his shoes. "Breakfast is in thirty minutes. I'll see you in the dining tent." He looked like he'd been up for a while already. His face was freshly shaved and his hair was still wet.

We groaned loudly to let him know we were awake— including Anna and Rachel on the other side of the curtain divider.

Bruno reminded us *not* to forget our program binders, and then left the tent to see Rudi.

I fought my way out of my mosquito net and went over to Eric's cot. He still looked pretty ashen, but that didn't say much about his health—he was always kind of pale. "How do you feel?" I asked.

He pushed back the white netting that made him appear even whiter and sat up cautiously. "Hungry, but otherwise okay."

"You should feel okay," Anna said from the other side of the canvas wall. "You slept for almost twelve hours."

"Really?" He looked at his watch. "Man, I don't remember anything."

Anna, Rachel, and Ben came over to Eric's bed.

"Do you remember the camp nurse coming here after you threw up the second time?" Anna asked.

"Not really," Eric said slowly.

Anna nodded. "Nurse Angelina said you might be delirious."

"Did the nurse say what's wrong with him?" I asked. "Does he have malaria from all the mosquitoes around here?"

"No," Anna said, "it's nothing like that. She said he either ate too much, got overheated, or a little of both."

"Well, I feel okay now." Eric slipped on a T-shirt. "And like I said, I'm starving."

"I hope you're ready for a story too," Ben said, "because we got a good one."

Anna nodded enthusiastically and grinned knowingly at Rachel. "Yes, Eric, you will enjoy their story."

I suspected that Rachel had already told Anna the highlights of our adventure last night, and that confirmed it.

Eric's eyes grew big. "I can't wait to hear what you guys saw down by the dock."

"What we saw by the dock," Ben said, "isn't nearly as interesting as what we saw in the jungle on the other side of the Panama Canal."

"You're kidding me!" Eric said. "Now I'm really curious about what I missed last night. But I think I'll enjoy hearing about it even more *after* breakfast. I gotta eat something... and soon."

"You might not want to hear about the leeches," Anna said, "with a full stomach."

"You saw a leech last night?"

We all thought that was kind of funny and laughed.

After going to the washroom buildings and quickly washing our faces and brushing our teeth, we hurried back to the tent, grabbed our binders, and scurried off to the dining area. Eric said he was healthy, but I could tell by how slowly he moved, he wasn't totally himself yet. Nurse Angelina saw us enter the big tent and walked over to intercept Eric.

"If you don't feel up to it, Eric," she said, "you shouldn't be out of bed."

"I feel okay," Eric said, "I'm just hungry."

"Are you sure?" the nurse asked. "Because I can make arrangements to have food brought to your tent."

"Really?" he said, but then he looked at Ben and me. I think he was tempted to relax another day, but he also didn't want to miss out on any more adventures with us. "Thanks—I'll be all right."

"Okay," she said, "but don't work too hard today. And drink plenty of water."

Eric grinned at us when she left. "You guys are my witnesses. She ordered me *not* to work too hard."

"She also said you can go back to bed and stay in a hot tent all day," Rachel reminded her brother.

"I'm not *that* sick." Eric moaned and rubbed his stomach. "I'm only partially sick."

"So to review," I said, "you're fit enough to eat and do whatever fun stuff we do, but you're too sick to do any archaeological work—like digging."

"Exactly!" Eric shouted, beginning to pile food onto his plate. "And that includes doing homework, by the way. I shouldn't do anything that might overwork my brain and make me delusional again."

"I think you mean *delirious*," Anna corrected.

"See," Eric whined, "all this heavy thinking is already confusing me."

Bruno joined us ten minutes later and explained that our team and the American team—Ben's original team— would have another orientation lecture right after breakfast. We put our trays away when we were done eating and went back to our table. All the other teams dispersed, heading to the dig site to do stuff, but we had to wait patiently for another boring lecture.

Rachel suddenly elbowed Ben. "Look," she said, "it's the police."

We all watched as four very serious-looking Panamanian police officers approached the dining tent. Three stayed outside while the fourth came into the tent to fetch Bruno and the other team leaders. The officer approached our table and explained in broken English that the police wanted to meet with all the archaeologists and team leaders, and Bruno should follow him to the artifact storage tent.

"Please wait here," Bruno said to us. "Perhaps you can begin on the book assignments while I'm gone."

When the adults had left, I looked around to see if anyone could hear us. It was safe. The American team was several tables away and already engrossed in their work binders.

I turned to Anna. "I wonder if we should have told your dad what we saw last night."

"Never mind *Bruno*," Eric said. "Tell me what *I* missed."

Anna ignored Eric and frowned. "Then I will be in trouble for lying to him. Papa doesn't like lies."

Eric tried again. "What did you guys *see*?"

Ben ignored Eric too. "But there's not that much to tell, Cody. We saw some people digging holes—that's all."

Rachel added, "If we start blabbing now, the camp director might restrict our movements or assign us a chaperone, and then we really wouldn't be able to do any more investigating. Plus, Anna might get grounded for lying. Don't forget, she was lying to cover for us."

"Can someone please tell me what the heck happened last night?" Eric begged.

So we did. It took about fifteen minutes of explaining and re-explaining, but in the end I think Eric had the whole story.

"So whatever they were trying to bury over there," Eric said, "Captain Pescada and Elvis are in on it."

"For sure," Ben said.

"And it looked to you guys like they were digging lots of holes to find the perfect spot to bury something." Eric continued to summarize our adventure. "And those holes were being dug near the same stone petroforms we have at home."

"Do you think those are the same people who stole the crystal skulls from the camp?" Anna asked.

I shrugged.

"At first," Rachel said, "we were absolutely convinced they took them. But now... now I'm not so sure."

"And what's with that yacht that was spying on the *Balboa*?" Eric said. "Could the people on that boat be involved in the skull theft too?"

Ben and Rachel shrugged.

We tossed around various crazy theories for almost an hour, until Bruno finally returned. He was with the assistant camp director.

"I'm sorry, children," Bruno said, standing over our table. "But we will have to postpone this morning's archaeological work in the dig. The police want to conduct a thorough search of the tent city, and they have asked that the team leaders accompany the investigators."

"What are we supposed to do all morning?" Eric asked, sliding the salt and pepper shakers back and forth on the table.

"After you complete Assignment #1 and #2 in your workbooks," Bruno said, "I suppose you are free to do what you like." He looked at the assistant camp director for confirmation.

The man nodded. "If you enjoy canoeing," he said, "you may take the camp canoes out on Lake Gatun. There is a nice little beach around the point, to the northwest. But don't forget to wear the life vests provided."

"Right," Bruno said. "And please stay away from the canal traffic and Mr. Anton Zola's yacht—he values his privacy."

"What?!" I cried. "He's here?!"

CHAPTER 8

THE ASSISTANT CAMP director frowned at my rudeness and moved on to speak with the American team.

"Mr. Zola's in Panama?" Eric said, thumping the pepper on the table.

Bruno frowned. "Did I not mention Mr. Zola?"

"You told us he might be spying on you," Rachel said, "but you never said he was going to be here."

"No," Eric said, "we would have remembered that."

"But I must have told you," Bruno said. "In Sultana. After meeting with your parents."

We shook our heads vigorously. *No way!*

Bruno now looked like *he* might throw up. He stared at his daughter for support. "Did I not tell you that another set of pillars might be in the area?"

"Yes, Papa," she said, "you told us about the pillars."

"And did I not mention Mr. Zola could be here too?"

"No, Papa."

"I'm ... I'm sorry," Bruno said, sounding truly sorry. "I meant to tell you he might be here. I suppose I forgot."

"It's okay," Rachel said.

"Yeah, it's not really that big a deal," I lied. "It was just a surprise—that's all."

Eric resumed playing with the salt and pepper—sliding the containers from hand to hand. "Considering what you told us, I'd be surprised if he wasn't responsible for stealing those artifacts."

Bruno shook his head. "I don't believe so."

"But then why is he here?" Eric asked.

"The company he owns, Zola Global, is a major financier of the canal expansion," Bruno said. "The project will cost five billion dollars and he is investing one billion."

Ben was trying hard to make sense of everything he heard. "So that guy in the fancy boat—this Mr. Zola dude—is here to keep an eye on the canal expansion work."

"Yes," Bruno said. "The expansion project is just as complex as the original canal excavation. It is reasonable to think that he would want to ensure the project remains on schedule."

"So he's probably not too happy," I said, "about the delay caused by the discovery of the skulls."

"Not at all," Bruno said. "When he first heard that crystal skull fragments were discovered, he was the one who ordered all work to be stopped so that the site could be properly examined."

I looked at Rachel.

Rachel went, "Hmmm…"

Bruno shuffled from foot to foot and looked relieved when the assistant camp director came back to our table to fetch him. Bruno waved goodbye and left the dining tent with the assistant camp director.

"I'm guessing," Ben said when we were alone again, "that you guys are suspicious of Mr. Zola."

I nodded.

"I'd bet anything," Eric said, banging the salt into the pepper shaker, "that he's somehow involved in this crazy skull business."

"Yes," Anna agreed. "It's much too much of a coincidence that he is here at the same time that two important artifacts are stolen."

"Anyone who prowls around at night with a infrared night vision light is a shady character, as far as I'm concerned," Ben added.

I didn't say anything, but I thought Ben's comment was kind of funny, because that's exactly what we were doing last night.

"That's for sure," Eric said. "He's definitely on Lake Gatun for more than just watching bulldozers push mud around—he's up to something."

I sat quietly, listening to my friends and watching Eric play with the salt and pepper. Then it suddenly hit me. "Wait a minute!" I cried.

"What's up?" Eric asked.

"I think we got it all wrong—we have it backwards."

"How do you mean?" Anna asked.

I grabbed the salt and pepper shakers from Eric and asked Ben to pass me another pepper shaker from his end of the table. "What if," I said, making a triangle on the table with the three shakers, "the people we saw last night weren't *burying* a treasure? What if they were *looking* for a treasure?"

"Sure," Ben said, "that's possible. They were digging lots of holes."

"Let's pretend these are the three pillars on the other side of the canal." I pointed at the shakers. "And—"

"But there were only two pillars," Ben said.

"Exactly," I said. "But we have similar stones in Canada, and there are *three* pillars in the formation. The centre of the three stones was used by ancient people as an astronomical marker."

"Kind of like Stonehenge?" Ben said.

I nodded. "Now, what if a hundred years ago, or a thousand years ago, or even ten thousand years ago someone wanted to bury something—something super important? Even if you had no idea what the pillars' purpose was, you could use the stones to help mark the spot—to help you find the location again. Right?"

"Yes," Rachel hissed.

"Of course," Anna said.

Eric frowned and ran his fingers through his blonde hair. "So how does that help us?" he asked. "You said those guys dug tons of holes and found nothing."

` I grinned. "That's because they didn't know *where* to look."

"And you do?" Ben said.

"If you knew the centre of those three astronomical markers was somehow very important," I said, "where would you bury a treasure—a treasure that you or someone else could find again?"

Ben pointed to the centre of the triangle formed by the three shakers. "I suppose I would bury something right here."

I pulled the salt shaker away from the two pepper shakers. "I think those guys are digging hundreds of holes because they don't know there were three pillars originally."

"Of course," Anna said. "They know that something is buried near the stones, but they don't know exactly where. They're just guessing."

"And they're guessing," I said, "because they don't know that there used to be three markers and one of them vanished. It probably slid down the hill, or got buried in a landslide, or whatever."

"If you're right," Rachel said, "the thing they're looking for can only be hidden in one of two locations."

"How do you figure that?" Eric challenged.

Rachel took my salt shaker and placed it on the table to form a triangle again. "If the third pillar was here, then they should dig here." She pointed at the centre of the three shakers.

Ben lifted the same shaker from the table and formed a new triangle. "And if the stone used to be here, then that's where they should dig."

Rachel clapped her hands together. "That's brilliant, Cody. That has to be it."

"I know it looks like the theft of the skulls from Camp Gatun is linked to what's happening across the canal," I said. "But whatever they're digging for by the pillars may have nothing to do with those artifacts."

"How about this for a theory," Rachel said. "What if sneaky Mr. Zola, or one of his henchmen, stole those broken crystal skulls from the camp and buried them across the canal? He probably knows there were three pillars, so maybe he instructed his men to stash them in the centre—the centre formed by the three pillars. And what if Captain Pescada saw Mr. Zola or his men near the pillars with shovels? The captain could be digging around because he's curious to see what Mr. Zola hid."

"There's only one way to resolve this," Eric said.

I nodded. "We have the whole morning free. I say we go over there and quickly dig two test holes. If I'm wrong, that's okay, but at least we'll have tried."

"And if you are right," Anna said, "we can clear Uncle Rudi's name and recover the stolen artifacts, or maybe find some other treasure."

Eric grinned. "And either way, we'll be heroes."

"We even have approval to use the canoes this time," Ben smiled, "so we don't have to be sneaky about taking them."

"All right then," Eric said, "let's go for a paddle on the world famous Panama Canal."

We left our workbooks on the table, walked out of the dining hall, and headed through the tent city toward the dig. On the way we saw five more police officers. They ignored us because they were focused on searching a tent—I think it belonged to the team from Brazil. When we got to our tent, Ben, Rachel, and I ducked in, grabbed our filthy clothes from the night before, and wedged them in Rachel's backpack. We didn't need the cops asking why they were so filthy.

On the hike from our tent down to the dock, we passed lots of older kids doing work at various locations around the site. Some were digging or using trowels to carefully scrape away layers of earth. Some were taking photographs or writing notes in journals. And others were using computers and GPS equipment to map out the area.

"I hope no one else is using the canoes," Eric said when we were halfway through the ancient village.

"Yeah," Ben said, "I sure don't feel like swimming to the other side."

Anna noticed an area that was being excavated by one of the teams, but there was no one around as we neared. She casually grabbed two shovels leaning against a wooden table and continued down the trail with us.

"Good thinking," I said.

Five minutes later we were staring down the hill at the dock. The *Balboa* was gone. It wasn't on our side of the canal and it wasn't on the other side, so it was likely making another run to Panama City to pick up people or supplies.

"Excellent." Ben pointed at the canoes. "They're all still here."

We dragged two of the four boats down to the water and put on our life jackets.

Eric snapped the clasps on the colourful vest together. "I better sit in the middle and take it easy." Rachel opened her mouth but Eric stopped her before she could protest. "Remember, Rachel, the nurse said I shouldn't do anything strenuous because I could get really sick and die."

Rachel snorted and shook her head, not wanting to start a silly debate with her brother.

"You realize," Ben said, "that if that yacht is still parked around the corner, they'll see us paddling to the other side."

"That's a risk I'm willing to take," Rachel said. "I'm never going into that jungle at night again—and I mean *never!*" She shuddered, probably remembering the leeches.

Rachel and I climbed in one canoe with Eric in the middle, and Anna and Ben hopped into the second boat. A rusty old freighter was about to navigate the tricky turn from the canal onto Lake Gatun, so we paddled a few tight circles close to shore to give it time to get out of the way. The tired old heap was taking forever, so I stopped paddling, pulled out my filthy T-shirt and dirty shorts from the night before, and began rinsing them in the warm water of Lake Gatun. Ben and Rachel saw what I was doing and did the same. By the time the ship had cleared the area, our stuff looked pretty decent again.

We wrung out the wet clothes as best we could and headed straight across to the jungle on the other side.

"Hey!" Ben shouted when we were half way. "Look!" He used his paddle to point at the shiny, bronze-coloured yacht, still floating where we saw it last night.

Eric took his binoculars from Rachel's bag and studied the craft. "Wow!" he whispered in awe. "You guys weren't kidding. That really is a fancy boat."

"You see anyone on it?" I asked, still paddling slowly.

"There's no one on the decks, as far as I can see," Eric said. "But that doesn't mean anything. Ten people might be watching us right now from behind all those mirrored windows."

I shuddered at the thought and tried to focus on getting to the other side before another big ship showed up. Our canoe slid up on the far shore a few seconds after Ben and Anna's.

"We won," Anna teased.

I laughed and said, "That's because you weren't bogged down with a lump of dead weight."

"I think you mean *sick* weight," Eric fired back. "I'm not dead yet."

We dragged the canoes high up on the muddy bank and left our life jackets on the seats.

"And this is where you saw the *Balboa* last night?" Anna asked.

Ben nodded. "Yeah, she was tied up right here... to that tree. And we found them digging the holes about ten minutes up the hill."

Ben and I each grabbed a shovel and led the way into the jungle, the others followed. After fighting through the thick shrubs that lined the shore, we checked ourselves quickly for leeches. The dozen or so we did find were easy to flick off because they never had time to latch and begin sucking our blood.

Beyond the dense trees of the lake front, the jungle opened up. It was a lot less spooky during the day. The sun sparkled through the gaps in the canopy high above us, and dozens of different birds shrieked at us for intruding in their forest. A few monkeys decided to join the protesting birds and howled insults from the branches overhead.

"What a racket!" Ben said.

"SHUT... UP... ALREADY!" Eric yelled at the top of his lungs.

"Shhh," Rachel hissed. "You want everyone to know we're here?"

Eric looked at Rachel like she was nuts. "This is a jungle, Rachel. There's no one here except noisy birds, crazy monkeys, and... and Tarzan."

"Tarzan lives in Africa," Ben said, "not Central America."

"Tarzan is fictional," Anna said. "He doesn't live anywhere."

The monkeys and birds got tired of yelling at us, or realized we weren't a threat, and calmed down. It was almost like someone muted the jungle volume, because the area suddenly became peaceful again.

I heard Anna whisper to Rachel, "This place is amazing... and beautiful."

Rachel agreed. "This is way more fun than sneaking around at night. But make sure you stay away from bushes, shrubs, and other low plants—they're covered with leeches."

We wound our way up the slope and stopped when we reached the holes.

"Holy cow!" Eric said. "What a mess!"

"They must have dug a hundred," Anna said.

I studied the many holes that covered the area. There was no order or pattern I could see—just a mess of random pits. Some of the holes were a metre deep, others only shallow dents on the jungle floor. It looked like they gave up digging and moved on to start a new hole any time they hit a root or rock.

"There's one of the pillars," I said, pointing to a stone column poking out from under a bunch of ferns.

"And there's the other one," Eric said. He jumped over a hole and headed to the second astronomical marker.

"The third pillar would have been around here," Anna said, stopping and using her body to from a triangle with the other two stones. "Or, straight across from me over... over there." She pointed to a spot between the markers.

Eric walked to the second possible location where the third pillar might have stood.

"Okay," I said. "Anna and Eric can stay where they are and we'll pace out the pillars to make sure they're standing in the right spots. Then, all we have to do is find the two centre points of the two triangles and dig."

Ben worked on the triangle formed by Eric, and Rachel helped me make sure that Anna was standing where the missing marker might have been. I counted ten paces between the stones that were still standing, which Rachel confirmed with her strides. Then, we each started at one of the pillars and began walking toward Anna. Her initial guess of the missing stone's location was pretty close. I moved her body back one pace and we measured again.

"Perfect," Rachel said, when she finished walking the triangle a second time. "All three sides are ten paces."

I estimated where the centre of the triangle might be and stuck my shovel in the ground. "Does this spot look like it's in the middle?" I asked Anna.

She nodded.

Rachel ran and looked over the top of a pillar. "Move the shovel back one foot," she said. "Toward Anna."

I moved the shovel and waited for Rachel to confirm the alignment using the third marker. The ground where I stuck the shovel, in the centre of the three pillars, was untouched. *Excellent*, I thought.

Rachel grinned at me over the stone. "That looks good."

Next, we helped Ben triangulate the centre point of the triangle formed by Eric. That one was trickier because several thick trees blocked our sight lines. We ran around checking and re-checking for several minutes until we were finally all satisfied. There were no holes near the shovel stuck in the centre of that triangle, so we now had two untouched spots to investigate.

"Good enough," Eric shouted. "I'm tired of standing around."

"Does that mean you want to be the first to take a turn digging?" Rachel asked her brother.

"I'd like to," he said, "but I'm not allowed—I'm sick."

We all laughed at that, including Eric.

Ben didn't waste any time. He grabbed the shovel and began digging into the soft moss and overburden that covered the ground. Suddenly he stopped and looked at the four us. "Is it just my imagination," he said, "or are you guys scared of the centre of these markers?"

I suppose I hadn't realized it until then, but we were all subconsciously avoiding the spot where Ben was digging.

We weren't going to tell him the truth, of course—that if you stood in the middle at the wrong time, you could vanish into a wormhole—but I had to say something. It's not that I didn't trust Ben with the information; it's just that if we told him what happened to us in Sultana, he might think we were all nuts.

"Ummm," I began. "We've heard a lot of rumours about these stones. And I suppose they do give us the willies a bit."

"What kind of rumours?" Ben asked, handing me the shovel.

"Nothing too specific," Rachel cut in, "just wild stories about magic."

The last time I stood in the middle of three similar pillars, I vanished into a wormhole and travelled forward in time to the present. But that was only because a full moon occurred at the same time as a summer solstice. I didn't think any unique astronomical events were taking place exactly then, so I took a deep breath and kicked the shovel into the wet earth. Nothing unusual happened— *thank goodness*—and I rapidly deepened the hole.

Rachel went over to the other spot we marked and replaced the shovel with her backpack. She carried the shovel over and helped me work my hole.

"My turn," Anna said, enthusiastically taking my shovel as soon as I paused to catch my breath.

Our strategy of using two shovels and taking short shifts was working perfectly. The hole deepened and got bigger right before our eyes. In fact, it was now just as big as the other holes that dotted the area.

But still no treasure, and still no missing skulls.

"Maybe we should try the other spot," Ben suggested after his fourth turn digging.

I nodded. "We could always come back to this hole later... I mean, if you guys want." I was beginning to think my entire theory was wrong. I had thought for sure we'd have more luck at the spot we were excavating.

Rachel remained optimistic. "Don't worry, Cody. We might still find something over there." She pointed at her backpack.

Anna studied the location where the third pillar would have stood. "It actually does look like a better spot," she said. "See how much lower that area is—the area where the missing marker was. The stone likely slid down the hill and got buried during a heavy rain or mud slide."

We dragged the shovels over to our second possible location and began digging. After watching us work for several minutes, Eric took the shovel Ben was using and shooed Rachel from the hole. "Nurse Angie will probably give me heck for doing this, but I can see you guys need my help."

We stood around the crater and caught our breath while Eric shovelled earth from around the thick roots that crossed in every direction. He did a great job deepening the hole, and the heaps of earth around the rim swelled rapidly. But after five minutes, even Eric looked exhausted.

"You better take it easy," Rachel cautioned.

"Yes," Anna agreed. "Let one of us take a turn."

CLUNK.

We all froze.

The blade of Eric's shovel had struck something hard.

"Did you guys hear that?" Eric looked over his shoulder at us.

We all nodded.

Eric gently double-tapped the soil in the bottom of the hole.

CLUNK. CLUNK.

He threw his shovel from the crater, narrowly missing my shin, and dropped to his knees. Eric prodded the loamy earth with his fingers. I watched as his shoulders stiffened. "No way," he whispered.

"What is it?" Ben said.

"Don't joke around," Rachel ordered. "If it's just a dumb rock..."

"It's not a rock," Eric said standing again. He turned around to show us something in his hands. "It's a crystal skull!"

"Wow!" Anna gasped. She reached out and carefully poked the top of the skull with two fingers, like she had to make sure it was real.

Eric passed the skull up to me.

I shook my head and pushed mud from the creepy eye sockets. "I can't believe it," I mumbled. "I can't believe we found something so..."

"So unbelievably important," Ben added.

I passed the head to Ben using two hands. "Careful... it's pretty heavy."

Ben eagerly took it from me. "Yeah," he said, enjoying the weight of it. "It must be a real crystal skull. If it was plastic it wouldn't be this heavy."

Anna held the skull next, while Rachel poured the rest of a water bottle on it. Together, they rubbed and rinsed the head until it was clean.

"We're going to be rich," Eric said, taking the skull from the girls again. "Filthy rich!"

"I don't know about rich," Ben said, "but famous for sure."

Eric held the skull over his head and screamed, "YAHOO!"

I heard the crunch of a branch down the hill and turned quickly. Anna and Rachel heard it too and whipped around.

"What was that?" Rachel whispered.

I squinted into the jungle. "I don't see anything."

"Is someone watching us?" Anna asked.

"The way Eric keeps yelling," Rachel said, "half of Camp Gatun could be here by now, watching us."

Eric and Ben ignored our paranoia and continued to admire the skull.

"You know what this place is, don't you?" Eric said to Ben. "It's a pet cemetery."

Ben considered that for a few seconds and nodded. "Could be," he said. "You guys mentioned this place might have magical powers."

Rachel shook her head. "Don't be stupid, Eric. This isn't a pet cemetery."

"It's the only possible explanation," Eric said.

"I don't understand," Anna said, "What do pets have to do with any of this?"

Rachel tried to explain. "We saw a movie about a pet cemetery where all the dead pets came to life again—and they were healed."

"Exactly," Eric said. "Whoever stole the broken skulls from camp buried the pieces here. And because this place is like that pet cemetery in the movie, the crystal skull is now fixed."

"I know it sounds pretty far-fetched," Ben said, "but it's perfectly logical."

Anna looked at Rachel and me to see what we thought.

Eric and Ben's theory sort of made sense. "But this area wasn't touched," I reminded them. "There was no sign of any digging."

"That could be," Ben said, "because the area healed itself *after* they buried the stolen pieces."

131

Eric nodded. "That's why they had to dig so many holes to find what they buried. They got confused because the spot looked different."

I didn't really buy that, but I couldn't offer an alternate explanation either.

"If that's true," Rachel said, "where's the second skull? Two broken skulls were stolen, so if they buried all the pieces, there should be a second skull here, in the hole."

Ben and Eric hopped in the pit so fast they almost bashed their heads together. They rooted through the damp earth with their hands like excited puppies. Mud flew in all directions for several minutes. This time it was Ben who suddenly stopped digging. He paused, pressed his face against the spot he was working, and said, "I think I found it."

I heard Anna mutter, "This can't be possible."

Eric twisted and helped Ben pry something from between the roots. It was impossible to see what they had. All we could do was wait and listen to them pant from exertion.

Eric began laughing like a madman. "It's the second skull! It really is!" He leaned back in the mud and caught his breath.

A few seconds later Ben placed a skull next to the first skull. He gave Eric a high-five and sat on the edge of the hole.

Rachel fell to her knees and examined the second head. "This is impossible!" she said.

Eric was still huffing but managed to say, "It's just like in *Pet Cemetery*, Rachel. I was ... I was right."

"The bad guys stole two *broken* skulls," Ben said, giving Eric a knuckle bump, "and we found two *fixed* skulls."

"And you will now give them to us," a stranger's voice called from up the hill.

CHAPTER
9

"HUH?" ERIC SAID, looking up the slope.

Two people were standing between the stone pillars, only ten steps from us. It was the girl and the guy we saw last night—I was sure of it. They wore shorts, T-shirts, and rubber boots. The boots made them look kind of funny, but the machetes they held in their hands made them look dangerous.

Ben jumped up, turned around, and looked in the direction we were staring. "Like heck," he said. "We're not giving you anything."

"You got that right," Eric shouted, standing defiantly beside Ben. "We found them, and we're keeping them."

Both strangers seemed startled by Eric and Ben's brave front. The young man—he didn't look anything like Rudi, by the way—stared down at the girl, like she was the decision maker. She frowned at her partner and then walked a few steps closer.

"Yes, you found them," she said, speaking with an accent. "But you found them on our land."

"These skulls aren't yours," Rachel said. "You stole them from across the river, and we're going to bring them back."

"We need them to prove my uncle is innocent," Anna added. "He has been accused of stealing them, when it was you."

"What?" said the young man. "We did not steal anything. These skulls have been here for hundreds of years."

I decided to join the debate. "Then what happened to the two skulls that were stolen from Camp Gatun?"

The girl didn't say anything. She lifted the straw cowboy hat she was wearing, ran her fingers through her straight black hair, and set the hat down again. I wasn't positive, but I thought they were both local Natives.

"And," Eric said, "what were you doing here last night?"

The tall guy said something in a strange language to the girl in the cowboy hat. She twisted her mouth and seemed to be considering what to do next.

"We are going to take the skulls," Anna said, "and we are going to leave now."

"Yeah," Ben added, "and if you make a ruckus about it, we'll go straight to the cops."

When Anna and Rachel began packing away the skulls, that really alarmed the strangers.

"You ... you can't go," the girl said, suddenly sounding more scared than angry.

"Just watch us," Eric said. He strapped on Rachel's now-heavy backpack and led the way down the hill with Ben right behind him.

The girl dropped her machete and ran up to me—I think because I was closest. "Please," she begged. "Please do no not take our skulls. Something horrible will happen to us—to everyone in the world."

That caught us all off guard.

Even Eric stalled and turned around. "But they're not *your* skulls," he said.

She grabbed my shoulders and shook them violently. "Please listen to me," she said. "Hear our story and what I have to say. Then, if you still want the skulls, they are yours—I swear it to you." She looked in my eyes with such an intense energy, I had to trust her.

"I don't feel like hearing a story," Ben said, "especially from a thief."

"We stole nothing," she insisted. "*You* are the thieves—taking sacred Chocoan artifacts from sacred Chocoan land."

I looked at Rachel and Anna, but neither one said anything. Maybe they were starting to feel guilty too. *Were we really the bad guys?* I wondered.

Eric sensed I was about to do something dumb. "Come on, Code," he said, "let's get back and show everyone what we found. Let's free Rudi."

The girl yanked on my arm again. "Please, listen to our legend," she said softly. "Please." I watched a tear slide down her cheek and decided I had to hear her out.

I turned to Eric. "Let's just hear what she has to say."

Eric groaned and kicked a rotten log. The wood disintegrated into a pulpy mess.

"Don't be such a baby," Rachel scolded her brother. "What's the big deal? She's only asking us to hear a story."

"The big deal is," Eric said, "that we finally solved a crime and found a cool archaeological artifact, and now she's trying to mess everything up."

The girl stood up straight and proud. "Are you an archaeologist," she challenged Eric, "or a greedy treasure hunter?"

Eric didn't say anything.

"A real archaeologist," she went on, "would want to know the story behind the artifacts he has found."

Ben sighed. "I guess it couldn't hurt to hear whatever local legend is behind the skulls. Maybe we'll be more famous if we know all the facts."

"Okay, okay," Eric said, "but why do I have the feeling we're going to be leaving this place without our skulls?"

The girl smiled at me. "Thank you," she said. "My name is Lucia, and this is my cousin Diego."

Eric and Ben walked back up the hill and joined us.

"Please follow me," Lucia said.

"Whoa!" Eric cried. "We're not going anywhere with you."

I didn't like the sound of that either. It was way too easy to get lost and disoriented in the jungle. "Why can't you just say what you want to say here?"

"Our village is right there," she pointed north, "perhaps a ten minute walk. Everything will be easier to understand if you see our home."

"How do we know you're not tricking us and that it's not a ten *hour* hike?" Ben asked.

Lucia thought about that. "If our village was that far away," she said, "we would not have heard you yelling from the stones."

We all looked at Eric. "What?" he said.

"Duh!" Rachel said. "Lucia and Diego heard you yelling and then came here to investigate."

"The jungle also told us," Diego added.

"The *jungle* told you?" Anna asked.

"Yes," Lucia said, leading us all north along the ridge. "The birds and monkeys and frogs let us know that people were near the sacred stones. You only have to listen to them."

Diego followed his cousin, and we followed the two Chocoans. I was behind Anna and Rachel, and Eric and Ben were behind me. As we rounded a corner, I held up my hand and signalled Ben and Eric to stop.

"If we sense a trap," I said, "or if it seems like they're trying to get us lost, we need to be ready to make a run for it."

Ben had been making up the rear, and he nodded vigorously. "I'm going to do my best to memorize the way back," he said, "in case—in case things get weird."

"Things are already pretty weird," Eric said. "I still can't believe we're following these strangers deeper into the rain forest."

Diego and Lucia continued to lead us through the jungle. They walked silently and confidently, occasionally swinging their long blades to whack a branch out of the way. After five minutes of hiking, the rough path we were on merged with a proper trail—a trail that looked like it was used regularly. And that trail slowly became a rutted road, which took us right into their village.

We all stopped in front of two dozen houses clustered together along a dirt road. An old jeep and few motorcycles looked like the only vehicles in town. The houses were made of wood and metal and looked reasonably solid. A power line that followed the road from the east jumped from house to house.

Eric whispered, "I can't believe there's a little village tucked away in the jungle."

I nodded. It really was a surprise.

"Where does that road go?" Anna asked Lucia.

"It goes east for thirteen kilometres," Lucia said, "and then south along the Panama railroad line. But we live off the land and the lake, and rarely leave town."

"And you have electricity?" Ben said.

"Of course," Diego said, "we need it for the lights and water pumps and refrigerators. Also, we can't check our email or use computers without electricity."

Lucia took us past a shabby building that we knew was a school. We could see (and hear) about twenty kids reading a passage together from a book. The door looked like it was about to fall off and none of the windows had bug screens. The teacher gave us a smile and a wave and then kept reading.

The next house was Lucia's, and she took us inside. The house was neat and clean but sparsely furnished.

"Please sit," Lucia said, pointing at an odd assortment of chairs around the kitchen table.

She took off her hat and hung it on a peg. The wall around the peg was covered with family photographs. One or two were framed, but most were just taped or pinned to the rough surface. I was studying one of the pictures when I heard Lucia say, "My father is at work, and the rest of my family is fishing on Lake Gatun and will not return until evening."

Eric didn't want to hang out in her house—he wanted to get right to the point. "Tell us what you want to tell us," he said.

"Please sit," Lucia said again.

Eric took off the backpack, sat down, and clutched the bag close on his lap. He wasn't going to let it out of his sight.

"How did you know where to find the skulls?" Lucia asked sitting down at the table with the five of us.

"You first," Ben said. "Why should we give you the skulls?"

140

She twisted her mouth again in that same funny way and began her story. "The people in this village—the Chocoan people—have sworn they would protect those skulls for the past five hundred years."

"Protect them from whom?" I asked. "Or what?"

"We were asked to keep them safe, until the right time."

"Who asked you to keep them safe?" Anna said.

"Tell them," Diego said. "They have to know."

Lucia looked at each of us for a second. "You will not believe what I'm about to tell you, but it is the truth—I swear it."

"Just tell us," Eric said. "We gotta get back."

"The story passed from Chocoan generation to generation states that a long time ago a strange man magically appeared at the sacred stones. He wore futuristic clothes and looked different from any of the other tribes on the isthmus."

"You're right," Ben said, "that's kind of hard to believe."

Anna, Rachel, Eric, and I glanced around the table at each other. Lucia's story may have sounded crazy to Ben, but it was perfectly believable to us because we had already used the wormhole marked by the stones twice.

"What exactly did this stranger want?" Rachel asked.

"The man presented our people with a crystal skull and said we must keep it safe for eight thousand moons. He said that when the time is right, the world will know why it is important."

"Maybe the right time is now," Eric suggested. "You've kept it safe—way to go—and now we're going to present it to the world."

"No!" Lucia cried. "We have done the calculations many times, and it is too soon. We are very close, but another forty years must pass."

"What's the difference?" Ben said.

"May I please see the skulls?" Lucia asked.

Rachel elbowed her brother, and he reluctantly took both skulls from the backpack and placed them on the table in front of Lucia.

Lucia didn't touch the crystals; she just stared at them and cried quietly for a minute. "The Chocoan have always protected the skulls' secret," she said, wiping her nose on her wrist. "But no one has seen the skull in over five hundred years."

Eric pushed both skulls closer to Lucia, indicating that she could hold them if she liked.

Rachel gave Eric a tiny nod and smiled.

"Why are there two skulls?" I asked.

Lucia continued to gaze at the crystals but still wouldn't handle them. "Around the time that the Spanish came to the area, a Chocoan artisan began to have visions. In his dreams, he was told to create a second skull—a skull that would be needed to trick a great foreigner into leaving the Chocoan alone. That artist broke several skulls before finally creating an exact copy of the skull the stranger brought. We don't know why the copy was never used. Perhaps the foreigner died before it was needed."

"Did your people have a village on the other side of the canal?" I asked.

"Probably," Lucia said. "The Chocoan constantly moved their communities around Lake Gatun." She finally picked up a skull and slowly examined it. "It's beautiful... flawless."

I looked at my friends. "That would explain the two broken skulls that were found across the canal at Camp Gatun—the ones Rudi is accused of swiping."

"*And*," Rachel said, "it would also explain why we found two crystal skulls by the pillars. One was the original skull and one was the copy made by the carver who had the dreams."

"But you have to admit," Eric said, "my pet cemetery idea made sense at the time."

Rachel grinned. "At the time, yes, but not anymore."

I tried to go back to Ben's earlier question. "I still don't understand why we can't show the world these skulls now."

Lucia gently put one skull down and picked up the other. "The man who appeared by the sacred stones was very specific and insistent. He said that if my people kept the skull safe until the right time, the entire world would benefit from its secret. But if the skull ever got into the wrong hands, the traveller said, all of humanity would suffer. Diego and I have been using our computer to calculate the time that has passed since the story first began. And eight thousand moons will have come and gone forty years from now. That is when we can give the skulls to science and to the world—no sooner."

Anna pointed at the crystals. "I wonder what they could possibly reveal *then* that they can't reveal *now*?"

"It must have something to do with the silicon," Ben suggested.

Lucia nodded. "That's what Diego and I believe too."

"Huh?" Eric said to Ben. "What do you mean?"

"Well," Ben said, "my dad is always talking about silicon wafers and silicon computer chips, and how they're the basic components in the memory of a computer."

Now I was confused. "I don't get it."

"These two crystals are in the shape of human skulls and look super cool," Ben said. "But they're still just giant chunks of quartz. And quartz is silicon—the stuff used to store information in all computers. The skull might be a massive memory chip."

"Yes, exactly," Lucia said. She sounded pleased that Ben understood. "Perhaps in forty years, humans will have the technology to read what is stored in these skulls, but until then we must keep them safe."

"The skulls might have information we need to cure a future disease," Anna suggested.

"Or maybe," I said, "they're the blueprints for a space ship to get to some other planet."

"Yes," Lucia said, "it could be anything like that."

"How come you were in such a panic to find the skulls now," Eric said, "after so many years?"

"As soon as we heard about the canal expansion," Lucia said, "we knew we had to find the skulls, so we began searching for them. We worried that this side of the canal would be widened too. If that happened, the sacred stones would be destroyed with the skulls. And when the area on the other side of the canal became an international archaeological site, finding the skulls became even more urgent."

"What difference did Camp Gatun make?" I asked.

"If the site over there were to become protected through international pressure, *all* digging would be moved to this side."

Anna's forehead wrinkled in thought. "So you were digging near the stones last night to try to find the skulls."

"Yes," Lucia said. "The people in our village have been taking turns searching for weeks. But after many days of hard work, people had to get back to work—to feed their families. Diego and I were the only ones left who still had faith in the prophecy; however, even he was beginning to wonder if the story was... was just a story. But now this... It was all true." She pointed at the two heads.

Eric grinned. "Yup," he said, "it's a good thing we found these guys for you."

"How were you able to locate them so quickly?" Lucia asked.

"We know something very important about your sacred stones," I said. "Something that helped us find the skulls."

Lucia raised her eyebrows. "What could you possibly know of our two stones?"

"Well for starters," Eric said, "There used to be *three* stones."

That really got her attention. "Three?" she said.

I explained to her that we had similar stones back home and that there were formations just like it all over the world. When I told her that we simply triangulated the centre of the two possible formations and dug our holes, she smiled.

"You are truly world-class archaeologists," Lucia said.

"So now what?" Eric asked, still comparing the two crystals.

"Well," Rachel said, "we can't take the skulls from here. Not now. Not after what Lucia told us."

"I was afraid of that," Eric griped. "She gets two crystal skulls in perfect condition, and we don't even get the broken ones."

"And to make matters worse," Ben said, "the cops still think Rudi pinched those broken skulls."

"I believe I know who stole the artifacts from Camp Gatun," Lucia said.

CHAPTER 10

"YOU DO?" ANNA asked.

"Yes," Lucia nodded. "I think the man with the expensive boat has them."

"The bronze boat sitting behind the point?" Ben asked.

Lucia nodded again.

The five of us suspected Mr. Zola might be involved, but it was interesting to hear a stranger had the same theory. "Why do you think he stole the crystals?" I asked.

"My aunt Bella delivers fresh fish to Camp Gatun each morning before sunrise. Yesterday morning she saw a man leave the rich man's boat and paddle to the shore in a black inflatable boat. She thought nothing of it, as she was also travelling on the canal very early. The stranger did not know it, but Aunt Bella followed the man through the jungle and up to the tents. She was not intentionally spying on the man. She was simply taking the same trails he took." Lucia laughed.

"What's so funny?" Ben said.

"My aunt Bella said the man moved like a bull. She said she could have followed the giant stranger blindfolded with all the noise he made. When they neared the tent city, my aunt became curious. She began to wonder why the man was clad in black and what business he had at Camp Gatun."

"What did she do next?" Anna asked.

"She tied her bag of fish to a tree and watched as the big man met one of the cook's helpers near the camp generator. Next, the helper—he is a young boy from Paraiso—guided the stranger into one of the tents and—"

"Which tent?" I said, interrupting her story.

Lucia shrugged. "I do not know and Aunt Bella did not say. Anyway, some time later, the man left that tent carrying a bag—a bag that appeared to hold something heavy."

"Hmmm . . ." Eric said. "That does sound like our perp."

"Our what?" Anna asked.

"Our perpetrator," Eric said, sounding very pleased to be explaining something to Anna for once. "The guy who committed the crime."

"Aunt Bella never followed the man back to the canal," Lucia said, "but she was sure he took something from the archaeologists."

"Then why didn't she tell someone at the camp?" Ben asked.

Lucia looked at Ben like he was loony. "Who would the police believe—a Chocoan fish peddler, or a wealthy man on a million dollar boat?"

"Would she step forward now," I said, "and tell someone what she saw?"

Lucia shook her head. "I'm sorry. We do not want trouble—not with the archaeologists, not with the Panamanian police, and not with those rich thieves. They can all make trouble for our little village."

"What happened to the boy—the cook's helper?" Rachel asked.

"The rumour Aunt Bella heard is that he complained of being homesick and was placed on the next canal shuttle home." Lucia grinned. "I suspect he and his family have been rewarded handsomely."

"Bribed, huh?" Ben said.

Lucia nodded.

"Hmmm..." That time it was Anna.

We sat quietly around the table for a long time, until Eric felt the urge to summarize our predicament. "So, Lucia gets both the good skulls, Mr. Zola gets the broken skulls, and Rudi goes to jail for stealing something he didn't steal. What a rip!"

"I'm sorry," Lucia said, standing up.

"That's not good enough," I said. "We helped you; now you have to help us."

Ben pointed at Anna. "Her uncle is about to go to jail because of your skulls. You have to talk your aunt into reporting what she saw. That might be enough to free Rudi."

This time it was Lucia who looked ashamed.

"If you don't help us," Eric said. "We'll be forced to spill the beans about these two skulls. I'm sure the

Panamanian government would be interested to know you have two of these ancient artifacts."

"All right, I will speak with Aunt Bella." Lucia said, heading for the door. "I will take you back now. But please don't do anything until I come to the camp."

When we got to the pillars again, Lucia begged us again not to do anything hasty and then walked away.

Eric watched her disappear into the jungle. "If I'd only kept my big mouth shut," he mumbled. "They wouldn't have heard me yelling, and we'd be the proud owners of *two* really cool skulls."

"We did the right thing," Rachel said. "If the Chocoan legend she told us about is true, we can't take the skull." She led the way down the hill and toward the canoes.

"*If* that legend is even true," Eric shouted at us from behind.

I don't think any of us were looking forward to the canoe ride back across the canal. We were all bummed. We had been excited about finding the skulls, but we had to leave those with Lucia. And just when we figured out who really stole the broken skulls, we couldn't prove it without Aunt Bella's cooperation. But that wasn't our only problem.

The canoes were gone.

We stood and stared at the black inflatable boat pulled up on the muddy shore.

"What the heck's going on?" Ben said. "The canoes were right here."

Anna pointed at the rubber boat with the small gas motor on the back. "This is the boat Lucia's aunt saw yesterday—the one from the yacht."

The bushes behind us suddenly separated and a monstrous man emerged from the forest. His face and arms were covered with scratches, and his dark clothes were soaked in sweat. He looked like he'd been prowling the area for some time. He smiled at us like he was pleased to have finally found us.

"What did you do with our canoes?" Eric demanded.

The man wiped his grimy forehead with his palm, but didn't say anything right away. I think because he had to catch his breath before he could talk. He had short black hair and a tan complexion, fitting Rudi's description perfectly.

"How the heck are we supposed to get home?" Ben pointed across the water to the dock. "This bozo took our canoes back."

I squinted over the water and saw our two canoes lined up on the shore with the other two canoes. *Well that's just great!*

The big man ignored Ben and pulled a leech from an arm that was as thick as a telephone pole.

"Hey!" Eric said. "We're talking to you. How are we—"

"I will take you back," he said with a heavy accent. We watched him pull off another leech and crush it under his heel.

"We're not going anywhere with you," Rachel said.

The big man sighed and pulled out a cell phone. He pressed a single button and waited. He talked to someone briefly and then passed the phone to me.

I didn't want to take the call, but my hand seemed to automatically reach for it. I held it to my ear. "Ahh... hello?"

"Is this Cody?" a voice asked.

"Yeah," I said, wondering how he knew my name.

"This is Mr. Anton Zola."

"Okay." I stared across the water at his yacht, wondering if he was watching me.

"Please get in the boat and let Krotek bring you here. I wish to invite you and your friends for lunch."

"We don't want to eat lunch on your boat," I said. "They'll feed us at the camp."

Mr. Zola paused and then said, "I would like to speak with you—with all of you."

"We have nothing to say to you," I said. "Now bring our canoes back, or we're going to tell the cops." I passed the phone back to the big man, who I guessed was Krotek.

As he listened to his boss, Krotek began scanning the many islands that dotted Lake Gatun. He said something into the phone in another language and nodded. Krotek pointed to one of the tiny islands two kilometres away, keeping his arm outstretched until we were all looking out over Lake Gatun.

"Was that Mr. Zola?" Eric asked.

I nodded. "He wants us to let this guy take us to his boat."

"No way!" Ben said.

"What's he pointing at?" Rachel said.

"Look!" Anna cried, pointing at the horizon.

A fireball, followed by a cloud of smoke, rose from the island. A second later we heard the explosion.

BOOM!

Krotek smirked and passed the phone back to me.

My heart was pounding so loudly, I didn't think I'd be able to hear anything. "Hello," I muttered.

"That island was uninhabited," Mr. Zola said. "But if you and your friends are not in that boat in three minutes, there will be another explosion."

I saw goosebumps appear on my arm. "What … wh …" I swallowed and tried to restart my mouth. "What does that mean?"

"It means that in three minutes there will be a similar *accident* in the kitchen at Camp Gatun. And it will be entirely your fault, Cody."

I passed the phone to Krotek.

"Get in the boat," I said to my friends. "This is serious." I think the tone in my voice told everyone I wasn't joking, because they all dove into the boat without arguing— even Eric.

Krotek effortlessly pushed the inflatable out into the water. The outboard purred to life after a single yank on the starter cord. Krotek twisted the throttle and we set off, plowing through the lake toward the gleaming yacht.

I quickly explained what Mr. Zola had said.

"What a lunatic," Ben shouted above the noise of the water slapping against rubber. "He can't go around blowing up islands."

"Well, he just did," Eric said.

"What could he possibly want?" Anna wondered.

"Maybe he's all worked up," Rachel yelled, "about those stupid pillars."

"I bet he wants us to show him where they are," Eric said. "Remember, Bruno said he's obsessed with them."

"Could be," I said, bouncing up and down on the wooden seat. "But I'm sure Big K here saw the stones when he went looking for us in the jungle."

Eric grinned. "I got it! He wants to use the pillars to try and fix the broken skulls he stole. He's using the same theory I had."

Rachel shook her head. "I doubt Mr. Zola watched *Pet Cemetery.*"

Eric shrugged. "You never know."

Krotek cut a wide circle around the point and pulled up behind the luxury cruiser. We bumped into a docking platform that extended from the rear of the boat, a foot above the water. I got out of the inflatable and studied the name painted across the stern: *Praise of the Two Lands.*

"Odd name for a boat," Ben said.

Eric nodded. "Yeah, I don't like it."

"You would prefer I named her *Obsession*, like every tenth boat in Florida?" We all looked up and saw a bird-like face peering down from the railing.

Rachel pointed at the transom. "What are 'the two lands'?"

"And who are you?" Eric demanded.

"The two lands are Upper and Lower Egypt," he said to Rachel. "And I am Mr. Zola," he said to Eric.

"What do you want with us?" Ben shouted.

He ignored Ben and said, "You are all welcome here. Please come up so we can discuss the matter inside." He disappeared from the railing, ending any further whining from us.

We climbed the ladder in single file and found ourselves on a beautiful open deck. The area had more couches and chairs than our entire house back home. A gold awning was pulled out overhead to protect everything from the sun. An attendant rolled a sliding door open for Mr. Zola and he went inside.

Krotek had huffed his way up the ladder after securing the rubber boat, and now he was shooing us from behind. "Inside. Inside." He waved his big arms at us like he was corralling a bunch of sheep.

"Relax, Big K," Eric said, looking around. "We're just admiring your boss's boat."

Krotek gave Eric a nasty stare.

"Don't make him mad," Rachel warned. "He looks like he could throw you clear across the canal."

Mr. Zola was wearing brilliant white robes, making it look like he was floating across the room. He sat down at the head of a long table. A lady walked over carrying a silver tray full of water bottles. She placed the drinks in front of the five empty chairs and retreated. We sat and waited for him to say something, but he didn't. After a minute of silence, another lady appeared carrying a white thimble in the middle of another shiny tray. I thought the thimble was a bit strange until I realized it wasn't a thimble—it was a tiny coffee cup. She set the little container it in front of Mr. Zola, bowed slightly, and backed away again. He grabbed the wee handle with two fingers and took a hamsterish sip.

Rachel and I looked at each other, and then we both looked at Eric. I'm sure we were both thinking the same thing: *Please don't say anything dumb.*

"Did you swipe that from some kid's play kitchen?" Eric asked, pointing at the cup.

Too late.

Mr. Zola slowly set the cup back down on a saucer the size of a quarter. "Excuse me?"

Rachel elbowed Eric under his armpit. "Please ignore my brother," she said. "What do you want from us?"

"I think you know exactly what I want. But, so there is no misunderstanding in the future, I will explain what I want. The crystal skull—the *one* you found at the petroforms today."

Eric said, "Which—"

He got an elbow from me that time for almost saying, "Which one?" If Mr. Zola didn't know there were two skulls, why should we go and tell him.

"*Which* we don't have," I finished for Eric. "We don't know what you're talking about."

Mr. Zola picked up his nursery school play cup and took another sip. After carefully wiping nothing from the corner of his mouth with a napkin, he snapped his fingers and said something in a strange language. Krotek lumbered over to the table from the sliding door he was guarding. Mr. Zola asked Krotek a question without even bothering to look at him.

The big man's arm shot out and he pointed at Eric.

"What?" Eric asked, trying to sound innocent.

Krotek explained something to his boss.

Mr. Zola nodded. "Krotek said he saw you all digging near the stone markers."

"So what?" Ben challenged. "We were looking for arti-facts—pottery and stuff."

Mr. Zola inhaled a slow, deep breath, and then let it out even slower. I got the feeling he wasn't enjoying our company. "Krotek waited in hiding to see what arti-facts you might find. He saw Eric lift a crystal skull from the earth, hold it high above his head, and shout with joy."

Eric pointed at Krotek. "So he came back here and told you I found a crystal skull—right after I found it?"

Mr. Zola nodded.

"What a snitch!" Eric said.

We all looked around the table at each other. Eric had just confirmed what we were all thinking: *Krotek didn't see Ben find the second skull.*

"Why should we give you the skull?" Anna asked, no longer pretending we didn't find one.

"As I explained on the phone, if you don't give it to me I will destroy the tent city at Camp Gatun. Boom!" Mr. Zola made a fist and then flicked out his fingers, demonstrating (I guess) what an explosion might look like if his ten skinny fingers blew up.

"You can't go around exploding things." Rachel said.

"Yes, I can," he said. "That island I blew up, for example, will not be given a second thought."

"But there are people at Camp Gatun," I said. "They'll get hurt."

"They most certainly will," he said. "And it will be your fault."

"We'll tell on you," Ben said. "It's five against one."

"True, but I gave the Panamanian government one billion dollars to expand the canal. You, on the other hand, did not. So in reality, it is one billion dollars against five kids. I assure you, the police will believe me."

"That's murder," Anna shouted.

Mr. Zola gave Anna an irritated look. "Twenty thousand people died when the canal was first built. I think if an *accidental* explosion today kills thirty or forty people, no one will be alarmed."

"You're crazy," Eric said.

"Perhaps," Mr. Zola said. "But I *will* have that skull."

I thought for a moment. "Okay," I said, "we'll give you the skull we found, but under one condition."

Mr. Zola couldn't resist a nasty smirk. "You are in no position to make demands, but I will entertain you. What is your condition?"

"We'll trade you the skull we *found*," I said, "for the broken skulls you *stole*."

CHAPTER 11

THE SMIRK VANISHED from Mr. Zola's face, and he began to turn red. "I... I have no broken skulls," he stammered.

Now it was Eric's turn to be a tattletale. "Then what did Big K... I mean, Krotek steal from the artifact tent yesterday at sunrise?"

Krotek's mouth slowly opened, but Mr. Zola silenced him with a quick hand gesture. He would definitely be going to bed without his supper tonight.

"I see I've underestimated you children," he said. "However, since you have been honest with me, I will now be honest with you. My business is that of rare antiquities, and there is nothing quite as unique as a genuine crystal skull. I confess—I did send Krotek to *borrow* the skulls. But upon testing... I mean, *examining* the skulls, they no longer have any special value for me. So I will gladly return them to you."

I shook my head. "We want Krotek to return them to Camp Gatun."

"Why?"

"Because everyone thinks my uncle stole them," Anna said quickly.

"Like you didn't know that," Eric said accusingly.

Mr. Zola didn't say anything.

"If Krotek brings the artifacts back," I said, "Rudi will be cleared."

"And if I agree to that," Mr. Zola said, licking his thin lower lip, "you will give me the crystal skull you found?"

We all nodded.

"But the thing is," I said, "we don't actually have the skull with us right now. We... we hid it again."

Mr. Zola squinted at us like he didn't believe that, or because he thought that was a stupid thing to do.

"You can check our bag if you like," Rachel said.

"That won't be necessary." He placed his palms flat on the table. "Cody will go and recover the skull, and bring it back to me. The rest of you will remain here and join me for lunch."

"We can't stay here," Anna said. "My father is expecting us back at camp."

"I'm afraid that's not true, Anna, because I spoke with your father less than an hour ago. I asked him for permission to invite you all for lunch, to show my appreciation for his contribution to archaeology. Your father thanked me and said I should remind you all to behave."

"Umph," Anna said, folding her arms and leaning back in the chair.

I cleared my throat and mumbled, "I'll need help getting the skull."

"Krotek will accompany you."

I didn't want the big guy along, but I didn't know how to argue the point. We couldn't risk him discovering there were two skulls and reporting that back to Mr. Zola. That wouldn't be good for Lucia, for the Chocoan, or for anyone on Earth. I mean, if that whole legend thing was true.

"It'll be a lot faster," Eric said, "if I go with him."

"*Faster,*" Mr. Zola said, "in what way?"

Eric slowly opened his water bottle, and then took his time drinking half of it. I knew he was stalling and trying to think of a good reason why he should be allowed to come with me. We all waited to hear what he'd come up with.

"Well, first of all," Eric began, "Krotek is out of shape. He's going to plow through the jungle like a big, stupid, sweaty, ugly cow. We hid the skull up the mountain and it'll take hours to hike there with him. He's useless... look at him."

Big Krotek didn't argue with any of that. In fact, I think I saw his head nod slightly in subconscious agreement. He probably didn't want to go back into the jungle either.

Mr. Zola continued to study his employee as Eric suggested. Maybe he was thinking about putting Krotek on a diet, or buying him a heavy-duty treadmill. Anyway, after watching Krotek for a minute (who was now looking at his feet, by the way), Mr. Zola turned to Eric again. "Go on."

"Plus," Eric said, "there are local Chocoan people all over those hills. We even saw a few hunters in the area. They'll hear *him* coming and take the skull from us long before we make it back here."

That sounded plausible to Mr. Zola and he nodded. "Then Cody must go alone. I do not want the skull stolen by local bandits."

Eric looked panicky—I think he'd run out of excuses—so I decided to help. "I have the best sense of direction in the forest," I said, "and I know where to go. But it was Eric who hid the skull when we got up the mountain. I was keeping lookout and I don't know *exactly* where he buried it. He has to come along."

"ENOUGH!" Mr. Zola shouted. "I am tiring of these games. Krotek will take you both across the canal. The two of you—and only the two of you—will go and get the skull. Krotek will wait by the water and guard the boat from locals. You have two hours." He stood up, straightened his robes, and turned to leave.

"Wait!" I said. "Does that mean we have a deal? You'll return the broken skulls if we give you the one we found?"

Mr. Zola didn't think that was worth turning around for. "I am a businessman," he said, with his back still to the table. "We have a deal, Cody. However, if you do not have the skull on this vessel in two hours... there will be—how shall I put it?—consequences."

"Two hours," Krotek said. He tapped the watch strapped around his meaty wrist, in case we didn't know what he meant. "Mr. Zola is not a patient man."

"Or a nice man," Eric mumbled as he climbed out of the inflatable.

I grabbed Rachel's backpack and followed him onto the muddy east shore, not far from the petroform site. "Just stay here and don't wander off," I said to Big K. "We'll be back as soon as we can."

For the third time in twenty-four hours, we battled through the shrubs near the canal and climbed the hill to the pillars. We didn't want to take any shortcuts and risk getting lost, so we decided to retrace our earlier route as best we could. When we got to the hole where we found the skulls, we took a break to catch out breath.

"I sure hope Lucia's home," I said.

"That'll be the easy part," Eric said. "The hard part will be convincing her to give us a skull."

I shook my head. "That shouldn't be a problem, because this is all part of her ancestors' prophecy."

"Prophecy?"

"Yeah," I said. "Remember what Lucia told us. A long time ago a man kept having a dream that he had to make a second crystal skull to fool someone—to trick some-one who would try and take the real skull. The Chocoan probably always thought they would need that fake skull to trick Spanish explorers or some looting con-quistador. But maybe this is exactly what was supposed to happen."

Eric considered that for a few seconds and then nod-ded. "It does seem like everything is going according to plan. The Chocoan have both skulls, Mr. Zola is the bad guy in the dream, and now they have to trick him with a phony skull. But... but we—"

"But we don't know which skull is the fake skull," I said, finishing Eric's sentence, "and which skull will save the world."

"That's going to be a problem."

We took off again to the north at a light jog. The twists and turns were still familiar and fresh in my mind, and I had no trouble copying the route we took that morning. We popped out of the jungle and onto the main trail a short time later. The path was smooth and well travelled, so I picked up the pace and ran for the village. The trees whizzed past me in a blur, and I just kept thinking one thing: *Please be home, Lucia. Please be home.*

Only she wasn't.

We pounded on the door of her house again and again. But no one answered. I twisted the door knob—it was unlocked—and opened it a foot. "Lucia! Hey, are you here?"

"Nuts!" Eric said, panting to catch his breath. "Now... what?"

An old lady came up behind us and said something in Chocoan or Spanish. I think she heard the yelling and needed to investigate. She gave us the same suspicious glare all senior citizens give teenagers and repeated what she said before.

I straightened up and tried to look like I wasn't there to steal food from her garden. "Lucia?" I said.

She frowned and shook her head.

I knew she wasn't around so I tried a different approach. "Lucia?" I said. I quickly pointed at the various houses in the community. Maybe she was in one of them.

Her frown turned into more of a scowl.

I tried a third time. "Lucia?" I pointed down the road to the east and raised my eyebrows. Then I pointed to the west, back down the trail we just took—the trail that went to Lake Gatun. "Lucia?"

The old lady nodded and said, "Lucia blah blah blah *Lago Gatun*." Well, she didn't really say the "blah blah blah" part, of course. But that's what it sounded like to us.

We nodded, said *Gracias*, and took off back down the trail to Lake Gatun. By the time we got to the turnoff to the pillars, my lungs were on fire. I knew the lake was somewhere up ahead; I only hoped it wasn't too far up ahead. Eric seemed like he had recovered from whatever ailed him the night before, but I was pretty sure this wasn't good for his health. I slowed to a walk and pretended that I needed a drink of water. To be honest, I really did need a drink of water, but I didn't want Eric to get dehydrated either.

"Man, am I hot," I said, digging out two water bottles. I passed one to Eric and guzzled half of mine.

Eric copied me and drank a bunch of water. "I sure hope Lucia's by the lake," Eric said. "Otherwise..."

I packed away the bottles, not saying anything. We both knew what *otherwise* meant. If we couldn't find Lucia, we couldn't find the skulls. And if we didn't get Mr. Zola his skull, he was going to blow up the tent city at Camp Gatun. I shook my head. *Does this kind of stuff happen to other kids?* I wondered.

We hurried on down the trail that wound through the forest and under the jungle canopy. Finally, after another half a kilometre, the trail opened up and we found ourselves in a small bay on Lake Gatun. But there was no sign of Lucia—or anyone else, for that matter.

"Rats!" I said, studying the odd assortment of boats and rafts dragged up on the shore.

"Do you think..." Eric wheezed, "do you think that old lady lied?"

"It's possible," I said, "but I can't imagine why." I looked out across the lake at the many islands. A long row of buoys snaked across the water and disappeared south around the point. I knew where we were now—we had cut across the point overland. If we followed the shore south and around the corner, we would eventually find Krotek swatting mosquitoes beside his inflatable.

"She must be fishing," Eric said, "somewhere out there."

A giant freighter poked its nose around the corner, and then straightened itself for the trip across Lake Gatun.

"We can't stick around here," I said, mopping the sweat from my face with my T-shirt. "We better go back and check with her neighbours again." I turned to go.

"Wait!" Eric cried. "Look!"

I spun around and searched for whatever he was pointing at to the north.

"There's a small canoe," Eric said, "coming at us... between those two islands."

"I see it!"

"I think it's her," Eric said. "Yeah, it's Lucia."

We both waved our arms and yelled for her to hurry. But that was a dumb thing to do, because instead of paddling faster, she stopped paddling altogether. She glided across the water and stared at us like we were nuts. We screamed and motioned with our arms that she should continue paddling—and *FASTER*. She got the message that something was up and leaned into her strokes.

Eric and I ran into the water up to our waists to meet her boat. Lucia remained seated while we each held one side of the bow steady.

"What is it?" she said. "What is the matter?"

I tried to explain. "The man in the fancy boat—the rich man—said he will blow up Camp Gatun if we don't bring him a skull."

"He can not have the skulls," she said defiantly.

"No, no." I tried again. "He doesn't know there are two crystal skulls. He thinks we only found *one* skull. We need to use the fake to trick Mr. Zola—that's his name, by the way."

Lucia's eye's looked like they were about to pop out of her head. "It is the Chocoan prophecy... The dream of my ancestor foretold of this day."

"Exactly," Eric said. "We need to give Mr. Zola that phony skull to protect the real skull."

She suddenly became panicky. "But we... But I do not know which one is the true skull."

"I know," I said. "That's why we need to go back to your house. We have to examine the skulls again. There must be something about the real skull that makes it unique."

She shook her head slowly.

"What?" I said.

Lucia quickly explained that she hid both skulls on one of the many islands on Lake Gatun. "How many days do we have to get him the skull?"

Eric and I stared at each other over the bow.

I studied my watch. "We've got one *hour*."

"Can we get to the island and back in sixty minutes?" Eric asked.

"No," Lucia said, "but I can ask my father to meet us at the island. He has a boat with a motor, and he can bring us back here very fast." She dug through the rucksack at her feet and flipped open a phone.

"You have cell phones?" Eric said.

Lucia began dialling. "Everyone has cell phones. Do they not have them in your country?"

"Well, yeah," Eric said, "but you live in... in a jungle and... Ahhh, never mind."

Lucia spoke to her dad in urgent tones. I didn't understand a word of it, but she repeated the words *Isla Carmelita* a few times. I suspected that was the name of the island where she stashed the skulls. She snapped the phone shut and said, "He will meet us there as soon as possible."

We dragged her canoe up on the bank and she pointed at another, larger boat. The three of us flipped the three-seater, slid it into the lake, and paddled like mad across the water. Lucia steered us north between the two islands and then farther east. After twenty minutes, our canoe banged into Isla Carmelita.

I knew right away why she picked the island. It was a graveyard. The ground was covered with hundreds of stone markers and tombstones.

Lucia grinned at our expressions. "Isla Carmelita is no longer used as a cemetery. It is considered haunted and cursed and evil. No one would dare come here and dig for treasures."

"Except you," Eric said, appreciating her logic.

"You're not superstitious?" I asked, jerking the canoe above the high-water line.

She shook her head and quickly tied the boat to a tree. "I'm more concerned about protecting the real skull." Lucia jogged through the ancient burial grounds. At the far side of the island, she stopped in front of a single moss-covered headstone that stood apart from the others.

"This is the spot?" I asked.

Lucia nodded, dropped to her knees, and began digging with her hands. "As children we often came here to scare ourselves—sort of a test, I suppose. Anyway, I was always drawn to this grave and the simple Chocoan symbols engraved on the marker."

Eric and I helped her scoop the earth away from the grave.

"What do the markings mean?" Eric asked.

"It says: CHIEF THIAGO—WISE AND BRAVE. That is all—no birth date, no death date, and no second name. The stone has always fascinated me. That is why I buried the skulls here."

A minute later we had the loose earth piled high around us and the skulls in our hands. At the same time, the sky opened up and poured rain on us. It was even worse than the rain that caught us on the canal the night before.

"This is insane!" Eric screamed above the noise of the rain.

"This is Panama," Lucia shouted. She calmly cleaned one skull using the water that spilled down on us. She passed me the clean crystal and began washing the dirty one. "Don't worry, the rain will stop soon."

Eric and I started examining the skull. But no matter how we twisted and turned it, we couldn't see any markings or features that made it unique.

"It looks perfect," Eric yelled.

"I know," I screamed back, "but does that mean this is the real skull, or a perfect fake?"

Lucia studied her skull from all angles and then traded heads with us.

"This skull seems foggier," Eric said, tapping our head. "The crystal in the other is clearer."

I nodded because I thought the same thing. "Yeah, but what does that mean?"

Eric shrugged. "Beats me," he said. "But we better think of something, cause we're running out of time."

As suddenly as the rain started, it stopped. The sun shone on Isla Carmelita and sparkled on the two skulls. Eric swapped crystals with Lucia and re-examined the clearer head.

"Let's go to the boat," Lucia said. "Perhaps Father is here. He may be able to help."

"What the...?" Eric whispered.

Lucia and I turned to Eric. He had his face mashed against the side of the skull.

"Did you find something?" Lucia asked.

"For sure... I mean, yeah, I think so."

"What was it?" I asked.

"I was trying to look through it," Eric said, "kind of angling it toward the sun, when I saw something inside. I think... If I can just hold it the right way again... Shoot, I lost it."

"Well, what was it?" I asked again. "What'd you see?"

Eric ignored me and continued to twist the crystal.

"We have to leave," Lucia said. "Father will be waiting down by the canoe."

"Just a sec," Eric said. "I know I saw... Come on, come on... THERE!" He froze and studied something inside the head.

Lucia and I held our breath.

"It's a picture of two people. And I think there's a rainbow too."

"Let's see," I said.

Eric passed me the crystal and showed me where to look. It took several tries, but I finally saw what he saw—a hologram of a man and a woman standing side by side. A three-dimensional image was suspended and locked in the crystal. I think the stress was really getting to me too, because the picture in the skull looked familiar.

While I showed Lucia where to look to see the hologram, Eric re-examined the other skull. After a few seconds later he triumphantly said, "Nothing! This has to be the fake skull."

We quickly agreed that true skull was the one with the images inside the crystal. Lucia placed it back in the water-filled hole next to the grave. The three of us pushed mud back into the hole and packed the earth as best we could. We raced through the cemetery and down to the water to meet Lucia's father and catch a ride back.

Only her father wasn't anywhere to be seen.

CHAPTER 12

I GLANCED AT my watch. "We're never going to make it back in time," I said. "We've only got twenty minutes. There's no way we can paddle across the lake, run down the trails to find Krotek, and get to the boat."

"We must try," Lucia said, untying the canoe. "People will die if that madman sets off an explosion."

"Hang on," Eric held up his palm. "I think I hear something—a motor maybe."

We waited as the noise of a boat coming from the north grew louder and louder. Suddenly, the *Balboa* roared around the corner at full speed.

Lucia waved her arms and yelled, "Father is here! He will help us!"

Eric and I stared at each other dumbfounded.

"Father?" Eric mumbled.

"Captain Pescada is your dad?" I asked.

Lucia continued waving her dad in toward us. "Of course he is. Did I not tell you that this morning?"

I was pretty sure I would have remembered her telling us that, but I let it go. We had more important things to sort through right now.

The *Balboa* pressed her nose against the muddy shore just long enough for the three of us to climb aboard. The second we were over the rail, Captain Pescada threw her in reverse and backed away from Isla Carmelita.

Eric and I followed Lucia across the deck to the wheelhouse. I didn't see Elvis around, so the captain had to stay at the controls. He slid down the giant window next to the throttles, and shouted something at his daughter. We had no idea what he said, of course, but I'm pretty sure it was something like, "What the heck's going on?" or "Why are these dummies with you?"

Lucia pointed toward the bay where we found her and screamed *deprisa*, hurry up. Captain Pescada aimed the tour boat in that direction and pushed the throttles to their stops. The bow rose high and out of the water as we left the island behind us. At first we plowed water and accelerated awkwardly, but once the boat gathered speed, the nose settled down, and we sped across Lake Gatun like a hundred-person speedboat.

I looked at my wrist watch. *Nuts!* We only had fifteen minutes to get to Krotek.

Lucia did her best to fill in her dad in on what was happening, while Eric and I stood behind her listening. His scruffy face went through all kinds of emotions as his daughter explained the situation. First he looked mad. That was followed by an expression of surprise. And then finally he became determined. I could tell he was determined, because he scowled straight ahead and wedged the stump of another one-inch cigar firmly in the corner of his mouth. He clamped down fiercely on the soggy mess as we forged ahead.

"We might still make it," Eric shouted above the noise of wind, water, and diesel motors. "But it's gonna be close."

I felt a glimmer of hope when I saw the Chocoan cove straight ahead between the two islands. But then the captain swung the *Balboa* wide and farther east. "Hey!" I yelled at Lucia. "What's he doing? The bay's right there."

"There is a reef between the islands," she shouted. "We will hit rocks unless we go around."

I looked at my wrist and groaned. *This wasn't good at all.* We needed every minute. There was absolutely no way we could run to Krotek in time. I had to do something before it was too late. So to show everyone I could be decisive too, I yelled, "Ummm... I think... I think I may have an idea. I mean, if you guys are okay with it, that is."

Captain Pescada ignored my decisiveness and kept the throttles gunned.

"What is it now?" Lucia shouted, sounding slightly annoyed.

"Forget about taking us to the bay," I said. "There's no time. Just tell your dad to drive directly to Mr. Zola's boat. It's our only chance."

Eric nodded vigorously. At least he supported me.

"But what about meeting Krotek?" Lucia asked.

I shrugged. "I don't think that matters, as long as we get the skull to Mr. Zola in…" I looked at my wrist. "In twelve minutes."

Lucia nodded and screamed at her father. The captain didn't hesitate. He threw the boat into a violent turn and cut across Lake Gatun—now aiming for the canal buoys that led to the Gaillard Cut and Mr. Zola's yacht.

After racing across the lake for a minute, Captain Pescada indicated Lucia should come into the wheelhouse. Once she had both hands firmly on the giant steering wheel, he left the controls and came out to talk to us, or yell at us—I wasn't sure which yet.

He studied us sternly and said, "Yesterday, I suggested you do not leave Camp Gatun. Did I not?"

We both nodded. I guess we were going to be yelled at.

"And today," he went on, "I find out that you violated the sacred stone site and found both the Chocoan skulls of legend." He lurched forward and embraced us both in a big, greasy, sweaty, cigar-smoke-smelling bear hug.

Eric and I groaned in shock and pain and revulsion.

"My people have obsessed over those skulls for generations. And my daughter…" He blinked away a tear that threatened to leave one of his bloodshot eyeballs. "Lucia has been searching for the true skull—to protect it—for a long time. You children have proven the legend is real and ensured that the prophecy will be fulfilled."

I nodded.

"You're... ahh... welcome," Eric said.

He ignored us for a second and tried to suck something tasty from his cigar. "You are like true Chocoans," he said. "You are clever, you are courageous, and sometimes you are stupid."

Eric looked at me and shrugged. "Thanks again... I guess."

"The special skull will continue to be protected," he explained (in case we didn't get that). "And the fake skull will finally be used to trick a powerful man. Everything is as it should be."

"As long as we get the phony skull to that boat," I reminded him, "*before* he starts blowing stuff up."

"Do not worry," Captain Pescada said earnestly. "You have saved our special skull; now we will help you and your friends." He took three quick puffs of his cigar and then studied what was left of it. He seemed surprised that the slimy tobacco leaves weren't burning—which wasn't a surprise to me—and flicked the butt into Lake Gatun.

The captain took the controls again, and Lucia joined us at the railing near the bow. The tour boat roared across Lake Gatun like she was built for racing—the bow lightly tapping each wave as it disappeared beneath the *Balboa*.

I studied my watch for the hundredth time. We were nearing the southern end of the lake and we had six minutes left. I knew Mr. Zola's boat was just around the point, so unless we ran out of gas, we were going to make it.

"There it is!" Eric shouted. "Straight ahead... About a kilometre away."

I looked at my watch again. "Perfect!" At the speed we were going we'd make it in less than five minutes.

"*Ay, caramba!*" Lucia cried.

I looked up to see the bulbous prow of a massive container ship slipping out from behind the point onto Lake Gatun. The fancy bronze yacht began to disappear behind the hulking ship. As more and more of the vessel blocked our path, it was clear we'd have to stop and wait for it to pass.

Only we didn't stop.

The *Balboa* screamed across the water on a collision course with the big ship. Eric and I automatically looked to the wheelhouse to check if the captain had abandoned ship. But no—Captain Pescada was still at the controls.

"What's he doing?" Eric yelled. "He can't play chicken with *that*." Eric pointed at the ship beginning to block the horizon.

"He will try to cut across her bow," Lucia shouted. Then, as if reading our minds, she added, "He knows what he's doing."

We watched in horror as Captain Pescada pushed our small tour boat across the container ship's path. I knew we were racing against the clock, but this ... this was nuts.

BOOOOOOOM!

The three of us jumped. For a fraction of a second I thought we were too late, and that Mr. Zola had blown up Camp Gatun. But it was just the freighter cursing our dangerous seamanship with an angry blast from its air horn.

The *Balboa* rode so close to the other boat, we actually passed under the shadow of the big ship's bow. I held my breath and waited for the crushing noise of metal against metal. But miraculously, we slipped across undamaged and shot out on the west side of the canal. Captain Pescada cut a gentle arc around the point and slipped in behind Mr. Zola's yacht.

Whew! We made it.

I'd seen how precisely Lucia's dad was able to handle the *Balboa*, so I was surprised when we bumped hard into the docking platform. The tour boat shuddered as it snapped the heavily lacquered planks behind the *Praise of the Two Lands*.

I looked over my shoulder at the wheelhouse. Captain Pescada grinned at me, shrugged his shoulders, and yelled, "Oops!"

"We will wait for you and your friends," Lucia said, "in case there is ... monkey business."

Eric and I nodded and jumped onto the damaged platform. The captain backed away slowly and idled in the small cove one hundred metres from the yacht.

I flung the backpack over my shoulder and scurried up the ladder behind Eric. We ran to the mirrored doors of the cabin, slid them open, and stormed inside.

"We got it!" Eric yelled. "Don't blow up anything. We have the skull!"

Mr. Zola sat in his chair at the head of the table, while Anna, Rachel, and Ben paced around the cabin impatiently. Everyone—except Mr. Zola, of course—ran over to us when we entered the cabin.

"Thank goodness," Rachel said, giving me an awkward one-armed hug.

"Man, you guys cut it close," Ben said.

Anna studied Eric. "Are you all right?" she asked. "You look terrible again."

"I'm okay," he said. "Just hungry."

Mr. Zola began clapping his hands—not in a happy way, but in one of those super-slow, creepy bad-guy ways.

We all looked at the table.

"Bravo," he said. "Now, can you all please sit? I would like to complete our transaction."

We took our places around the table again.

"I see you took an alternate vessel back," Mr. Zola said calmly.

"We ran out of time," Eric said. "We had to."

He nodded. "Very resourceful. May I please see the item?"

I opened my bag, pulled out the fake crystal skull, and placed it in front of Mr. Zola.

He gasped.

Rachel, Anna, and Ben gawked at the clean, shiny head, and then turned to Eric and me. Mr. Zola, meanwhile, continued ogling his prize skull. I wanted to let my friends know that we knew what we were doing, so I tried to give them a conspiratorial wink and a nod. But I think I messed that up because they still looked pretty worried.

Mr. Zola cleared his throat. "Please sign the documents," he said, "and you can be on your way."

"What documents?" I said.

Rachel pointed at two papers sitting in the middle of the table. I hadn't noticed them in all the excitement. "While you guys were gone," she said, "he had his lawyer email some sort of contract here to the boat."

"But what for?" I said. "I thought we already had an agreement."

"We do," said Mr. Zola. "However, upon reflection, I felt that we needed something a bit more... official."

Eric and I looked at each other. We had no idea what that meant.

"He wants us to sign a contract," Ben said. "And the contract says that we agree not to change our minds and try and get the skull back."

Mr. Zola nodded. "But it also states that I will have the two broken skulls returned to Camp Gatun."

"You mean the skulls you stole from the camp?" Eric asked cheekily.

Mr. Zola shook his head. "An employee of mine stole them, and I ordered that employee to return them."

"Don't you think," I said, "you should include something in the contract about removing the explosives from the camp?"

"There were never any explosives," he said. "I told you that simply to motivate you. I am a businessman, not a terrorist."

We all stared at Mr. Zola.

What a rich, sneaky jerk!

I considered what he said. "So that contract makes this all legal?" I asked. "Even though we're kids?"

He nodded. "The deal will be finalized when we all sign it."

I did a bit more considering. "I think," I said, again being very decisive, "that I would like to add one more thing to the contract."

"Huh?" Eric said.

Mr. Zola frowned. "You wish to add a clause?"

"Yes," I said, "I want to add a clause." I wasn't sure exactly what a *clause* was, but it sounded like the thing that I wanted to add. I continued: "You're going to get a genuine, priceless crystal skull—the only one in the whole world—and we're going to get nothing except the return of two broken skulls."

"That is true," he said.

"Well, this skull is Chocoan," I said, pointing at the crystal, "and I think you should do something nice for the Chocoan people. I want you to build a new school for their village. It's just across the water."

"And why should I do that?" he asked.

"So that you can keep their sacred skull," I said. "If you build them a school, we'll sign the contract and we'll promise to never tell the Chocoan, or anyone else for that matter, that you stole their skull."

Mr. Zola smiled. "I don't see what bargaining power you have. You are children. You can't do anything to stop me."

I stared back at him good and hard. He was right, of course, but I couldn't let him know that. We were a bunch of kids in a foreign country, and Mr. Anton Zola was a billionaire who seemed to have the power to do what he wanted. Sure, he was a liar and a ... *Wait a minute.* If he could bluff us, maybe we could bluff him ... again.

"That's what you think," I said, trying to sound like I wasn't about to make up a bunch of lies. "If we aren't back on the *Balboa* in thirty minutes, Captain Pescada and his daughter are going to get eighty Chocoan warriors. They're going paddle over here in their canoes, storm this boat, and then wreck everything until they find *their* crystal skull again."

Mr. Zola's smile faded a little bit. "And why would the captain not fetch the warriors now? I have the skull. He must know I will leave with it."

"He personally doesn't care about the skull, but his people do." I said quickly. "He knows the government will simply take it anyway and put it in a museum somewhere. He wants his people to benefit immediately, and what they need right now is a new school."

"Hmmm..." That was Mr. Zola.

"Plus," Eric said, "he thinks the skull is cursed, so he doesn't really care what happens to it. But the rest of his people will totally freak out on you when they find out you're pilfering their sacred skull. So there!"

We all suffered through another minute of silence, waiting for him to make some sort of decision. Finally, he said "Very well, Cody. That sounds reasonable. I will gladly build them a new school."

"You will?" Ben said, equally shocked.

"Yes," he said. "I will ask my legal team to make those changes and send a revised contract immediately."

I didn't know what to say, but somehow I managed to croak, "Good, you do that."

CHAPTER 13

"AND YOU'RE ABSOLUTELY sure you gave him the fake skull?" Rachel asked.

"For the tenth time," Eric said to his sister, "yes."

"I still can't believe you guys did all that in two hours," Ben said. "Man, I sure wish I could have come along with you."

It was 2:30 in the afternoon and we were all back in the camp dining tent sitting around our unopened binders. The place was empty, except for a cook who was checking his emails on a computer in the corner. Captain Pescada and Lucia had dropped us off at the main dock thirty minutes earlier. We knew we'd see the captain again, but Lucia hugged us and thanked us for five minutes before she let us leave the Balboa.

"That was nice of you to ask for a new school," Anna said, "for the children."

I shrugged. "It was the least we could do, I guess."

"I still think you could have demanded some stuff for us," Eric griped. "I bet he would have bought us video games and all sorts of cool gadgets—if we'd only asked."

"Don't be so selfish," Rachel said. "You should be happy Lucia's village still has their secret skull and will get a new school."

"I am happy," Eric whined. "But I'd be happier if I had a new dirt bike too."

We all laughed.

Bruno stormed into the tent with his brother right behind him. They were both grinning like they'd each won a dirt bike. "Ahh, good, you're all still here," Bruno said.

We all jumped up from our seats.

"Uncle Rudi!" Anna cried, running up to her giant uncle.

Still here? Eric and I looked at each other. *Mr. Zola must have lied about calling Anna's dad too.*

We each took turns greeting Rudi and shaking his hand.

"I have good news, children," Bruno said. "The stolen skull pieces have just been returned."

We pretended to be surprised.

"Who stole them?" Ben asked.

"Well," Bruno began, "it seems that one of Mr. Zola's deckhands—from his beautiful yacht—sneaked into camp and stole the artifacts. When Mr. Zola became aware of the theft, he ordered the man to immediately return the skulls and apologize."

"That is fantastic," Anna said.

"It's not so fantastic for the thief," Rudi said.

"Oh?" Eric said. "Why's that?"

Bruno took a few seconds to chuckle. "Mr. Zola was so appalled at his employee's behaviour, he ordered the fellow to spend the week here digging pits and trenches for the archaeologists. The hard work may not reform him, but he's certainly going to lose some weight."

"Huh," Rachel said.

"I believe I may have misunderstood Mr. Zola," Bruno said. "I think he is a gentleman and a great philanthropist."

"He collects dinosaur bones?" Eric said.

"What?" Bruno stared at Eric. "No, no, that is a *paleontologist*. Mr. Zola is generous with his money. We also just found out that he has moved a team of contractors from Pedro Miguel to a small village across the canal. They will be building a new school there for the local children."

"Wow!" I said.

"That was fast," Ben said.

"I'm sorry?" Bruno said.

"I mean," Ben said, "the stolen skulls were *returned* fast."

"Oh, yes." Bruno nodded. "Of course, of course."

He studied us carefully for a minute from the end of the table—sort of like he was seeing us for the first time. "You children are working much too hard," he said. "You need to go outside. The fresh air will do you all good, especially you, Eric—you look awful."

We promised we would take a break from our *intense* studying, and Bruno and Rudi left the tent again to go and examine the broken skulls. "We would like to take a good look at them before they are sent to Panama City," Rudi said on the way out.

As soon as they were gone, Rachel leaned forward, "Okay, tell us *exactly* what you saw inside the skulls, Cody."

"I think I can do even better than that," I said. "I can show you."

I left them in a state of confusion and walked over to the cook. He closed his computer and smiled at me. "Hallo," he said, using pretty good English.

I gave him what I thought was a sad, homesick look, and said, "Could I please use your computer for a minute to email my mom?" The cook said he didn't mind because he had to start making stuff for supper anyway. He opened the laptop again and showed me the basics. Three minutes later I was back with my friends.

"What're you doing?" Eric asked.

"Since we left the yacht," I said, carefully setting down the cook's computer, "I've been thinking about the image we saw inside that crystal skull."

"Was it freaky?" Ben asked.

"Well, yeah, it looked freaky," I admitted, "but it also looked familiar. In fact, I'm certain now that I've seen it before." I pulled the computer close and did a quick search for the image I wanted. The screen filled with dozens of photos of the two people we saw hidden deep inside the crystal. I clicked one of the images so that it filled the entire display. I spun the computer around and said, "*This* is what we saw."

"Holy cow!" Eric cried. "That *is* what was in the skull."

"What is it?" Anna said.

I tapped the computer screen. "This is a photograph of the plaque NASA bolted to the first spacecraft that ever left our solar system."

Ben nodded. "Pioneer 10, right? I remember our science teacher telling us about that."

"Yeah, we learned about it in school too." I turned to Rachel. "Remember when Mrs. Snedden showed us those slides?"

Rachel's brow creased like it always did when she was deep in thought. "Didn't she tell the class that NASA put the plaque on the spacecraft in case it was ever intercepted by extraterrestrial life? NASA wanted aliens to know what humans looked like, right?"

"Exactly," I said.

"You mean this is what you saw?" Anna asked, studying the laptop. "A man and a woman standing side by side?"

"Not exactly," I said.

"Huh?" Ben said.

"What we saw inside the skull," I said, "was a three-dimensional version of this—a hologram."

"Yeah," Eric said, "it was like this—a man and a woman standing next to each other—but with way more detail. It was totally in 3-D."

191

"With a rainbow," I said.

"There was a rainbow in the skull?" Anna said, sitting up a bit.

"Yeah," Eric said again, "right over the heads of the two people."

"Is a rainbow important?" Rachel asked Anna.

"Perhaps," Anna said. "It is the universal symbol of peace and hope. In mythology it is considered a bridge between two worlds. And in many cultures it represents water."

We sat quietly, listening to the distant kitchen noises.

After a minute, Ben cleared his throat. "So, let's see if we can work this out," he said. "Five or six hundred years ago someone showed up near here with a crystal skull. And inside that skull there was a hologram of the same image that NASA bolted onto Pioneer 10. But Pioneer 10 didn't blast off into outer space—*or even exist*—until hundreds of years later."

"That's the way I see it," Eric said. "But what does it all mean?"

"What if," Ben continued, "someone from the future wanted to let the world know that we weren't all alone in the universe? I know it sounds crazy, but what if a person from the future time-travelled to the past to help people... to give all mankind a hand with something?"

None of us thought that Ben's idea was crazy, because we all knew that the pillars opened up wormholes to the past *and* the future.

"If that's what happened," Eric said, "the secret Chocoan skull could be someone's way of saying 'Hello.'"

"And if their legend is accurate," Anna said, "the people who made the skull also included some special information inside it."

I nodded. "Too bad we have to wait until we're old to find out what that information is."

"That's fine with me," Rachel said, "as long as Mr. Zola doesn't get his hands on it or—"

"Or discover he has a fake skull," I added quickly.

"He can't possibly..." Eric said. "And anyway, he does have a *real* crystal skull."

"That's right," Ben agreed. "I mean, it's not like his skull is made of glass, or rubber, or recycled pop bottles. It is a real crystal skull—just not the secret crystal skull."

Rachel studied my frown for a minute and then said, "What're you thinking?"

"I suppose I'm worried that he knows there's a secret skull. He said something on the boat about *testing* the stolen broken skulls. What if he tests his skull and finds out it's only a slab of quartz?"

Eric shrugged. "All I know is," he said, "I wouldn't want to be around him if he ever does figure out we swapped skulls.

"If we are lucky," Anna said, "he will continue to think he has the only genuine unbroken crystal skull in the world. And the secret Chocoan skull will remain protected and hidden away." She paused and quickly repeated, "If we are lucky."

Anna was right—getting caught or saving the world all came down to us either being lucky or not being lucky. I know that could be said for many normal situations, except the shenanigans we found ourselves in were never normal. They always seemed to be really messed up and in need of luck—buckets and buckets of luck.

QUESTIONS for DISCUSSION

1. In the prologue, we meet Thiago and his grandfather and learn about the origin of the crystal skulls. Why do you think the author started the book so far in the past? Later in the story, were you surprised to learn where (and when) the original skull actually came from? Why or why not?

2. Imagine that someone has offered you the opportunity to travel to a faraway country and take part in an archaeological dig—but your parents don't want you to go! What would you say to convince them to let you go on the trip?

3. Think about the characters of Cody, Eric, Rachel, Anna, and Ben. Which one of the kids is most similar to you in terms of personality? Which one of them (if any) do you think you would be best friends with? Which one might you not get along with? Explain.

4. Dr. Bruno Wassler's brother, Rudi, is accused of stealing crystal skulls, even though he didn't do it. Have you ever been accused of doing something wrong that you didn't actually do? How did that make you feel? Did you defend yourself, or just let it go? Have you ever falsely accused someone else of something, either accidentally or on purpose? What happened?

5. Every country has archaeological sites that contain precious artifacts. Who do you think should get to decide what happens to those artifacts?

6. Sometimes archaeologists find really cool things, like the crystal skulls in the story, but most of the time, they find less-important things, like pieces of pottery or everyday objects like tools. Do you think it's important to study those everyday objects, or should they just be ignored? Why or why not?

7. Imagine that archaeologists five hundred years from now are on a dig, and they find your house! What items in your house, and especially your bedroom, might they find? And what do you think those items will tell them about you?

8. Have you ever seen a leech? What would you do if you had to walk through a leech-infested jungle, like Cody, Rachel, and Ben did?

9. Why do you think Mr. Zola agreed to build a school for the Chocoan village? Do you think he really cares about the community?

10. If you could choose between being an archaeologist like Dr. Wassler or a billionaire like Anton Zola, which would you choose? Why?

DISCOVER A WORLD
OF ADVENTURE WITH
THE SHENANIGANS SERIES.

Available now:

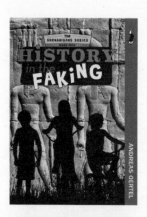
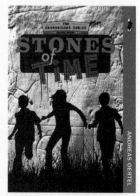
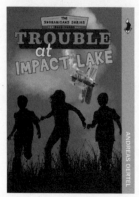

COMING SOON

In Too Deep

The Shenanigans Series, Book Five

When Cody and Eric are denied permission to recover golf balls from the ponds at the local golf course, they decide to trespass on the property and snorkel at night. But they end up finding a lot more than just golf balls. Hidden in the murky water they discover a life-size bronze statue of a man.

Perhaps the answers to this mystery should have been left to the depths...

ABOUT the AUTHOR

ANDREAS OERTEL WAS born in Germany but has lived most of this life in eastern Manitoba, Canada. He now lives with his wife, Diane, on the beautiful Lee River, near Lac du Bonnet, Manitoba.

Andreas has degrees from the University of Winnipeg and the British Columbia Institute of Technology, and a lifelong passion for archaeology, ancient civilizations, and writing, especially for young people. In addition to creating fun books for tweens, Andreas enjoys travelling, reading, watching movies, and exploring the great outdoors.

Andreas is the tallest writer in Canada (194 centimetres, or 6 feet 4 inches) and can be found exploring Manitoba beaches with his trusty metal detector, Lucky.

Visit andreasoertel.com to learn more about Andreas and the Shenanigans series.